W9-BHL-959

NPLF
Nashville Public Library
FOUNDATION

DISCARDED
From Nashville Public Library

ARCADE
AND THE TRIPLE T TOKEN

Also by Rashad Jennings

The IF in Life

ARCADE AND THE TRIPLE T TOKEN

RASHAD JENNINGS

ZONDERKIDZ

Arcade and the Triple T Token

Requests for information should be addressed to:
Zonderkidz, *3900 Sparks Dr. SE, Grand Rapids, Michigan 49546*

Library of Congress Cataloging-in-Publication Data

Names: Jennings, Rashad, 1985- author.
Title: Arcade and the Triple T token / Rashad Jennings.
Description: Grand Rapids, Michigan : Zonderkidz, [2019] | Series: The coin slot chronicles | Summary: Just before starting sixth grade in New York City, a stranger gives Arcade Livingston a necklace that sends him and whoever he is with on wild adventures. |
Identifiers: LCCN 2018045498 (print) | LCCN 2018051288 (ebook) | ISBN 9780310767404 (ebook) | ISBN 9780310767411 (hardback)
Subjects: | CYAC: Adventure and adventurers—Fiction. | Middle schools—Fiction. | Schools—Fiction. | Brothers and sisters—Fiction. | Magic—Fiction. | Bullying—Fiction. | New York (N.Y.)—Fiction.
Classification: LCC PZ7.1.J4554 (ebook) | LCC PZ7.1.J4554 Arc 2019 (print) | DDC [Fic]—dc23
LC record available at https://lccn.loc.gov/2018045498

Illustrated by: Alan Brown
Art direction: Cindy Davis
Interior design: Denise Froehlich

Printed in the United States of America

18 19 20 21 22 /LSC/ 10 9 8 7 6 5 4 3 2 1

From myself and that little overweight kid with glasses, asthma, a 0.6 GPA, and an impossible dream; and to all the present and future kids of the Rashad Jennings Foundation—

If there was one place I could grab you by the hand and take you right now, it would be to that day in your life when you finally decided in your heart that,

"No matter what it takes, I'm going to become the absolute best version of myself!"

Truly, that is when your own Arcade adventures begin. And may they never end . . .

Prologue

"Arcade, you can't have *all* those books!"

Mom tilted her head back to look at the tower of books I had arranged on the check-out counter at the Ivy Park Public Library. It resembled the Empire State Building, just a little shorter.

"But I need 'em, Mom." I flashed my brightest smile her way. "I'm interested in *all* these topics."

"And how are you going to carry them home on the subway?"

Ugh. The subway's a cool way to travel, but there's only so much room. And I only have so many arms. I frowned. "Okay . . . I'll take half."

Mom shoved a fist on her hip. "Arcade, you've got twenty or thirty books sittin' there! You can take *three*. That's all."

Oh, man. Three?

This was going to take some thought. I disassembled my collection and carried the first seven books back toward the children's section.

Ms. Weckles, the children's librarian, saw me coming.

"Arcade Livingston! You spent an hour picking those out. Are you changing your mind now?"

I shook my head. "Nope. Just can't carry them all. But don't worry, Ms. Weckles, I'll shelve these for you. I've been studying up on the Dewey Decimal System."

"It's a good thing." Ms. Weckles stood up and pointed her index finger toward the ceiling. "Because we all know, a misshelved book is a . . ."

"Lost book!" we said together. With a smile, Ms. Weckles sat down and went back to her work.

I rounded the corner toward the nonfiction 900 section: Travel. I reshelved the Switzerland guide book. I *really* wanted to explore those Alps. I patted the spine and pushed it in until it lined up with all the other cool travel titles. "Catch ya next time," I whispered.

"Excuse me, young man . . ."

I turned toward the weak voice to find an old, dark-skinned woman about my height, staring into my eyes. She wore a glittery silver-and-gold ballcap that said "Triple T" on it.

"Yes, ma'am?" I bobbled the books and had to bend to catch one that tried to escape the stack.

She grinned. "I see you like books."

"Yeah. A little too much. I gotta put these back." I stepped aside to make room for her to pass, but she just kept staring. And now it seemed like her cap was glowing.

"And did I hear your name right? It's . . . Arcade?"

"Uh, yeah. Arcade. I know it's unusual, but yeah. That's me." I flashed a smile and adjusted the books again.

"Then this . . . is for you." The woman reached up with her crooked fingers and removed a chain from around her neck. Before I could stop her, she dropped it over my head and around mine.

"What? Oh, no, I couldn't . . ." I bobbled the books again. She moved around me, as agile as a cat, and began walking away. Fast. "Wait!" I yelled. "What is this? Who *are* you?"

She stopped for a second, turned, and looked at me one last time. "Happy travels." She winked, gave me a thumbs-up, and then vanished behind the aquarium, her silver-and-gold glow radiating around the clownfish.

I dropped the books and sat down cross-legged in the travel section. A round object dangled from the end of the chain. I pulled it up to take a closer look. It was shiny gold—a brand-new arcade token. On the front side, toward the bottom, there were three Ts connected together. I ran my finger over the raised design. It sort of vibrated at my touch and, was it my imagination, or was *it* glowing? And then, it turned on its own! A surge of energy shot through me as I read the letters that curved around the borders of the top and bottom:

Arcade Adventures

Chapter 1
The Question

We're very impressed with you, Mr. Livingston. In fact, you're number one on our list to fill the position of sixth-grade teacher at Forest Park Middle School in the fall. We just have one more question to ask you to help us make our final decision . . ."

"Sure! What would you like to know?"

"Can you tell us . . . and this is really important . . . how many sides are on a stop sign?"

"That's the question?"

"Yes. It's very important."

"Ummm, yeeeah. Okay. That's an easy one. Stop signs are everywhere. I see them every day."

"Yes. How many sides? Please answer the question."

"The answer is . . . ten. There are ten sides on a stop sign."

WHOMP!

"OW!"

My eyes opened to darkness and the smell of a good book. That's because I had been reading while lying on my back, holding the book in the air. Then, like I've done a bunch of times before, I fell asleep and dropped it on my face.

Thump! Thump! Thump!

"Arcade! You better be up! You don't want to be late for the first day at your new school."

It was my sister, Zoe. She's in ninth grade and, just because she's older, she thinks it's her responsibility to pound on my door every morning and get me up for school.

"You only have fifteen minutes to get out the door, and you know Mom wants you to have a nutritious breakfast."

She also always says *that*.

I sat up and let the book—*Underwater Wonders: A Complete Dictionary of Marine Animals*—slide off my face onto my lap. A little bit of blood trickled from my nose.

Whew. Good thing it didn't get on the library book.

"Arcaaaaade!"

"I'm dressed, Zoe. No need to worry."

I flipped the sheets off me.

Good thing I slept in my clothes.

All I needed to do now—since it was Friday—was to put on a pair of my famous crazy socks, and I'd be ready to go. Well, that's not *exactly* true. I wasn't ready *at all*! Who starts their first day of school, in a new state, on a Friday? And on *March 26th*?

You do, Arcade Livingston.

I grabbed a tissue from my nightstand and stuffed it up my nose to stop the bleeding. Then I shuffled over to my desk. I scanned my school admission paperwork the secretary had printed out when we visited last week.

Arcade Alexander Livingston: 6th Grade, PS 23, Ivy Park. Room 603—Mr. Dooley.

PS 23? It sounded like a gaming system, not a school.

"Arcaaaaaaaade!!!"

"Zoe! Chill!"

"I will when I see you standing out here in the hallway."

I unzipped my black backpack with the pink flamingos and carefully placed the paper in my notebook. Then I grabbed my red-rimmed glasses off the nightstand and shoved them on my face. Okay, now I could see clearly to deal with my sister. I turned the knob and cracked the door halfway, poking just my head out.

"Hey, Zoe." I grinned the cheesiest grin I could. Then I frowned. "What happened to your hair? Looks like it got caught in a blender." I flashed the cheese again.

"Very funny, fish face. Happy first day of school." She pushed my door open all the way. "What happened to your nose?" She pulled the tissue out.

"Book battle," I said. "And I lost."

"Seriously, Arcade? You should use an e-reader." She looked down at my ankles.

"No socks? Isn't this crazy sock Friday?"

"Oh yeah, I forgot!"

I threw the backpack down at her feet and ran to my

dresser. It only took a second to make the decision. Today was definitely "jellyfish socks" day. I had just read about jellyfish before I fell asleep and was rudely interrupted by that silly stop sign dream.

Zoe counted as I sat down on my bed to pull my first sock on.

"One thousand one, one thousand two . . ."

"If you were a nice sister, you could use those seconds to get me a . . ."

A granola bar shot my way like a cannonball and hit me right in the Triple T token hanging from the chain I got from that mysterious old lady at the library. The granola bar landed on the carpet. I snatched the token in my fist and dropped it inside my shirt.

"Whatcha got there, bro?"

I picked up the granola bar, unwrapped it, and took a huge bite. "Mmmm. Chocolate chip. Thanks."

Zoe crossed her arms and leaned against the doorframe. "That's not what I'm talking about. What's up with the necklace?"

"It's not a necklace."

"Then what is it?"

I glanced up at my clock. "Don't we have to get out of here in, like, two minutes? You don't want to be late on your first day at your fancy-pants private high school, do you?"

Zoe stiffened and looked at her sport watch. "Okay, let's go. But you'll have to spill it about the necklace later."

We hauled our backpacks down the stairs of our brownstone apartment. My dog, Loopy, was waiting for us at the bottom. He's a Shih-poo. A cross between a Shih-Tzu and a poodle. But, basically, he's just a chocolate-colored, furry, licking machine. And on Fridays, he's confused, because he can't lick my naked ankles.

"Hey look, Loopy! Zoe's wearing sandals!" I picked Loopy up, gave him a rough cuddle, and set him down at Zoe's feet, where he wagged his tail and licked her toes.

"That's gross, Loopy." Zoe stood there, rolling her eyes. "Arcade, control your dog."

I grabbed him up and put him behind the gate in the kitchen. "Be good, boy. I'll be back after school. Try not to lick all the paint off the cabinets." Loopy just barked, slobber flying out in all directions.

On the dining room table sat two notes from Dad. One for me and one for Zoe. It's a good thing Dad's a note-writing guy. Since he started his new job as a set designer and stage manager on Broadway, he's been up all night for shows. Which also means that from now on he'd be sleeping until the afternoon and wouldn't be making our breakfast or seeing us off in the morning like he used to in Virginia.

This is what my "first day of school" note from Dad said:

> *Hey Bud, you've got this. Just hang on and enjoy the ride.*
>
> *Love, Dad*

I took a deep breath and showed Zoe. "*Enjoy* the ride? No one *enjoys* being the new kid."

Zoe patted me on the shoulder. "You'll do alright, Arcade. Everyone always likes you."

I sighed. "We'll see about that. What does *your* note say?"

She opened and closed the paper. "It says basically the same thing."

I stepped closer and reached out for the note. "Nuh-uh."

Zoe pulled the note away. "Okay, give me some space and I'll read it to you."

I backed all the way into the living room. "Is this enough?"

"Barely."

She shook her head, and I could tell she was trying hard not to smile. Then she began to read:

> *Dear Zoe,*
> *I am proud of you for taking a risk at this new high school. You have many talents, and I know that God is going to direct you exactly where he wants you to go. So be brave, and be Zoe!*
>
> *Love, Dad*

I adjusted the backpack on my shoulders. "So he tells *you* that he's proud and to be brave, but he tells *me* to hang on? Sounds like he's sending me off to the rodeo or something."

Zoe laughed. "You think too much. It's going to be a great day. You'll see."

"Whatever you say, blender head."

On the steps outside our apartment sat my only friend in New York City, Doug Baker. He lives just a few houses over from us. I met him a week ago at the public library. I was there reading books, as usual, and Doug . . . well . . . he was there looking for free candy. I'll never forget hearing his loud voice ringing through the place.

"Where's the free candy? I'm all in for THAT!"

Ms. Weckles was having a special promotion that day to get early sign-ups for the summer reading program. She had posters put up all over town that at the bottom in small print said: "All the free candy you can eat." Yeah, it was pretty clear from our first conversation that Doug and I were at the library for completely different reasons.

"Hey, dude, whatcha readin'?"

"A book about robotics," I mumbled.

"You say you're reading a book about robotics?"

"Yeah, that's what I said."

I tried to resume reading, but I was distracted by the sounds of a sucker clicking around in Doug's mouth.

"You like candy?" he asked, his words coming out muffled because of the sucker stick clenched between his teeth.

I still didn't look up, but nodded and said, "Some kinds."

"Some kinds?"

I slammed the book closed, leaned back in my chair, and stared at Doug for the first time. "Yeah, that's what I said."

And that's how it goes with Doug. If you ever forget what you just said, no worries. He'll repeat it back. Even if his mouth is filled with food, which it is, most of the time.

And today, on this morning of my first day of school, Doug Baker was sitting on the bottom step outside our brownstone, munching a big, fat blueberry muffin.

"Hey, Doug," Zoe said. "You here to help Arcade get to school?"

Doug swallowed. "You bet! First days can be gnarly." He jumped up and brushed a whole bunch of crumbs off his lap.

Zoe smiled. "That's nice. Do you mind if I walk with you two as far as the subway entrance?"

"You wanna walk with us to the subway entrance?"

Zoe crunched her eyebrows together. "Yeah, Doug, that's what I just said."

I laughed to myself as I checked my phone for the time.

"We better make tracks." I pointed to my phone screen, and Zoe's eyes grew wide.

"Oh no . . . we can't be late!"

We all jogged down my new street, around some random corners that I had not seen yet, through a couple of alleys, until we ended up at the entrance to the subway, where Zoe had to pick up a train going to Smartsville.

"Hey, Zoe," I bent over, hands on my knees, huffing and puffing. "Before you go, I have a question."

She laughed. "What's new? You're a question machine. Ask away."

"Okay," I took a deep breath. "How many sides would you say are on a stop sign?"

She was panting a little herself. "Are you *kidding* me?"

I shook my head. "Nah. I just want to know what you think."

She breathed in deep and put both hands on her hips. "A stop sign is an octagon, Arcade. And everyone knows an octagon has eight sides."

"Yeah." I looked at her, serious as I could be. "But it also has a front side and a back side. Doesn't that actually make ten?"

Zoe narrowed her eyes. "Look, if anyone ever asks you how many sides a stop sign has, you better say eight. You got that?"

"But it doesn't make sense, Zoe."

"What are you *talking* about? It makes perfect sense."

Zoe gave me an intense stare before she turned toward the subway tunnel.

"Octagon means eight, Arcade. Don't go thinking any other way. *Especially* on the first day at a new school."

My sister is a straight-A student. And she knows way more than I do—like how to speak French, how to identify any kind of bird in the wild, and how to bake the perfect cake. But the way she said, "Don't go thinking any other way," *annoyed* me so much that my body heated up like I was catching fire. I put my hand to my chest, and my jaw dropped.

It wasn't my *body* that was heating up. It was that Triple T Token. And it was burning a hole in my shirt!

CHAPTER 2

Mr. Dooley

The first thing I noticed about my new teacher, Mr. Dooley, was his voice. His *loud* voice.

"CLASS, PLEASE WELCOME OUR NEW STUDENT, ARCADE LIVINGSTON."

There was a little applause. Most of the students just stared at me. Probably because of the awesome socks. At least that's what I hoped. But the huge, identical-twin guys in the middle of the classroom were definitely *not* staring at my socks.

"What kind of a name is Arrrr-caaaaade?" one of them grunted out. His red polo shirt was all wrinkly, and his black, tight-curly hair had a funny dent in the front—like he'd been wearing headphones, took them off, and then sprayed lacquer on it to keep it in place.

"It's a cool name, Tolley," Doug said. "And Arcade lives on our street."

The other twin, who somehow had the exact same wrinkled shirt and dented hair, scowled. "Not on OUR street. I haven't seen him outside once."

"That's because he's in the library a lot," Doug said. "'Cause he's a bookworm."

Thanks, Doug. I'm sure the bullies will love to know that about me.

"WELL, ARCADE," Mr. Dooley continued to shout, "WE ARE HAPPY TO HAVE YOU HERE AT PS 23. TAKE WHICHEVER EMPTY SEAT YOU WOULD LIKE."

To save my eardrums, I took the empty seat *farthest* from Mr. Dooley, on the end of the very back row, next to a gentle-looking girl, who gave me a small grin and a half-wave.

"Hello, I'm Amber," she said, in a pleasant decibel range.

I smiled and sat down. "I'm Arcade."

She put her hand to her mouth and giggled. "Yes, I know. Mr. Dooley just said that."

I nodded. "Oh, yeah."

Nervous sweats attacked me right then. I grabbed the edges of my desk and held on.

Mr. Dooley continued, a little quieter. This time.

"Now that we have introductions out of the way, I am pleased to announce our sixth-grade spring project."

Mr. Dooley stood in front of the class, and now that I wasn't being blown off my feet by his voice, I was able to focus on him a bit. He was average-sized, with short, light-brown hair, parted on the side. Nicely dressed in tan khakis, a light-blue dress shirt, and gold-rimmed glasses. Unfortunately, I had to look between the twins' wrinkly red shirts to see him. The brother on the right turned back toward me and gave me the stink-eye. Then he bumped his brother's shoulder, whispered something, and they both laughed.

"Casey and Kevin, is something funny?" Mr. Dooley ripped his glasses off with one hand and crossed his arms. "I don't think I've told a joke yet this morning. But some good ones are coming, so PAY ATTENTION."

So, the wrinkly brothers had names. Casey and Kevin Tolley. But which one was which? Hmmmm. Didn't matter. They both looked like trouble to me.

Mr. Dooley continued.

"This year, our sixth-grade class will be putting on a career expo for the entire school. You will be working in teams of four, and you'll create displays, complete with information and hands-on activities that will teach the kids about jobs they might like to have when they grow up. THIS IS A COMPETITION, PEOPLE—THE WINNING TEAM WILL WALK AWAY WITH A VALUABLE PRIZE. Now, doesn't that sound like fun?"

"That sounds RADICAL!" a red-headed, freckly guy in the front section of the room blurted out, and *then* raised his hand. He moved a lot in his seat, like he was using the back of his chair as a scratching post.

"Yes, Mr. Scranton?" Mr. Dooley raised an eyebrow. "Go ahead, since you already spoke RADICALLY out of turn."

Mr. Scranton, who from this point forward I planned to call Scratchy, put his hand down but used it to scratch his head first. "Oh, sorry. Can I bring in a car engine and take it apart for the kids?"

Amber leaned over my way. "Sounds greasy," she whispered.

Mr. Dooley rubbed his chin. "That's something that would be interesting to lots of kids! Of course. Mr. Scranton, I LIKE YOUR ENTHUSIASM. I'll explain more after lunch, but for now, we're going to pick teams, and you can get together and decide on the careers you would like to explore."

I imagined me, Scratchy, Casey, and Kevin ending up on the same team. The freckles, the bullies, and me, the bookworm.

I shuddered at the thought.

Mr. Dooley picked up a large, glass bowl from his desk. It was filled with folded yellow scraps of paper. "I have added all your names to this bowl. Who would like to come and pick out the first four names?"

Doug popped up from his desk in the front and ran toward the bowl. "You say you want someone to pick out the first four names?"

"Yes, Doug, that's exactly what I said."

Doug grinned. "Okay, then, I'll pick out the first four names." Doug pointed his finger toward the bowl. "Hey, is Arcade's name in here?"

Mr. Dooley threw his hands up. "Oh, I almost forgot. Good call, Doug." He walked behind his desk, opened the top drawer, and rustled around. He pulled a red post-it note off a pad and wrote on it. Then he held it up for the class to see.

ARCADE LIVINGSTON.

He dropped the red paper into the clear bowl along with the yellow ones and mixed them up with his hand.

Doug laughed and reached in the bowl. He grabbed the red paper first, of course.

"Gee, I wonder whose name he picked?" Scratchy snorted and scratched his nose while he looked over at me. Everyone in the class laughed.

"Arcade," Mr. Dooley said, "you are the first member of Team Number One."

"You mean, Team Number *Loser.*" The Tolley on the left coughed out the word loser.

"Casey, that better *not* happen again," Mr. Dooley said as he shook the bowl to mix up the remaining papers. "Go ahead, Doug. Let's find out who the next three members of Team One will be."

Doug formed a V with his index and middle finger. Then he pointed at his eyes with the V. He turned it around and pointed the V back at me. "You and me, baby!" Doug reached in for a paper, opened it up, and read the name. "Bailey Martin," he said, and his shoulders drooped.

Amber leaned over my way again. "That's good, she's smart." Then she pointed over to a skinny, blonde girl seated in the second row, who had covered her face with her hands and was shaking her head.

"Looks like she really wants to be on my team," I said, and Amber laughed.

"Next one," Mr. Dooley shook the bowl.

Doug did the V thing again, and this time it worked, because he pulled his own name for Team Number One. "Yes!" He pumped his fist in the air. "Bookworm, baby!"

Doug! Quit saying that!

Doug danced around a little, and Mr. Dooley finally had to stick the bowl under his chin to get him back on task. "One more, Doug. We don't have all day." Doug reached in. I looked around the room at the prospects.

Please, God. No Tolleys. Please, God, no Tolleys. Please, God, no Tolleys . . .

"Amber Lin," Mr. Dooley announced.

I breathed a sigh of relief. I looked over at Amber. She was smiling at me, and her fingers were smacking together in a little baby clap.

Me, Bailey, Doug, and Amber. We were Team One.

No Tolleys. Maybe it wouldn't be so horrible after all.

I didn't hear the rest of the names being called. I just kept thinking about Dad's note:

Hang on and enjoy the ride.

What does that mean, Dad? If I have to hang on, how can a ride be enjoyable? Doesn't that mean it might be dangerous and scary? It just doesn't make sense.

Next thing I knew, the members of Team One had

dragged their chairs over to my desk, and Bailey started handing out booklets that said *Sixth Grade Project—Guidelines and Requirements* on the front cover. "It would be best if we read this whole thing by the end of lunch," she said. "And we'll have to exchange phone numbers and decide on some study times. I suggest we meet at the Ivy Park Public Library." Then she turned to me. "Do you know where that is, Arcade?"

"Ha!" Doug smacked me on the back. "Of course he does. I told you he's a bookwo . . ."

I reached over and clamped my hand over his mouth. "Yes, Bailey, I know where it is. And Ms. Weckles, the children's librarian, is awesome. She'll help us find whatever we need."

Bailey cracked a smile. "Ms. Weckles? She works here at our school library too. Okay then, Ivy Park Library it is." She jotted down notes in a thick planner. "Now, let's start with the first study question on page one of our booklet."

We all turned to it, and Bailey read, "What do you want to be when you grow up?"

Silence.

Bailey glanced around at the team. Doug and Amber's mouths hung open. Mine did too.

Bailey put down her pen, formed her hands into fists, and began cracking her knuckles. "Come on, Team One, this is *not* a good start."

Then, someone behind me sneezed in my ear. It was one of the Tolley brothers, and he sneezed out . . .

"Losers!"

Chapter 3

A Bumpy Walk Home

"What we need is a sweet team name," Doug said, as he walked backwards in front of me.

"No, what we need are some ideas of what we want to be when we grow up."

"We need some ideas of what we want to be when we grow up?"

"Yes, Doug, 'cause right now we have nothing." And that was stressful. Even after lunch, Team One couldn't come up with anything concrete during our brainstorming session. Poor Bailey had practically cracked her fingers clean off.

The only one who came close to anything was Amber, who kept saying, "Maybe something in the medical field."

"I think my idea of you being a Marine Biologist was genius. I mean, check out those socks!" Doug pointed to my jellyfish.

"Nah, I don't like swimming in cold, salty water. Other than that, it would be cool." I remembered my book, *Underwater Wonders,* and I reached up to press on my nose to see if it was still sore. Yep.

"What other socks you got? That could give us ideas." Doug turned back around, unzipped a side pocket of his backpack, and pulled out what looked like a ten-day-old donut. "Cha-ching! I forgot I had this!" He stuffed half of it in his mouth and chewed away.

"Maybe you should look into the food industry. Something like a chef . . ."

Doug licked the glaze off his fingers. "That could work. Or hey—how about food critic?"

I stopped, tilted my head back, and laughed out loud. "Critic? So tell me, how *is* that stale donut?"

Doug ripped a piece off. "Awesome! Ten thumbs up."

I started walking again. "Yeah, *that* won't work. Hey, how about competitive eater?"

This time Doug stopped. "That's a thing?"

"I think so. We can check it out at the library."

"Why don't you just Google it?"

"'Cause I have all kinds of restrictions on my phone."

Doug laughed. "Yeah, me too. I guess it's good I have a new friend who likes books! We're gonna come up with some great stuff. I'm glad we're on Team One together." Doug scrunched his nose. "Team One. It sounds *so* boring. We need a sweet name."

We walked a little bit longer, trying to think of things to be.

"Astronaut?" Doug said. "That would be out of this world."

"Ha. Ha. Ha. How about dog trainer? Loopy could use the help."

"Or pilot!" Doug pointed to the sky, but then frowned. "Except I'm afraid of heights."

"So why did you say astronaut? They go higher than pilots."

We joked with each other until we reached the subway station entrance where we left Zoe off that morning. Zoe was right there waiting for us.

"Hey, little brother! How was the first day of school?" Zoe's face was all bright and shiny, and the ponytail she always puts her hair into after school looked springier than ever.

"It was pretty good," I said. "I didn't get paired with any of the Tolley brothers for the spring project, so that's a win."

Zoe put one hand to her cheek. "Tolley? I met a Michael Tolley in one of my classes today."

Doug munched away on the other half of his donut. "Yeah, that's their older brother. He's really smart. And then . . . there's Casey and Kevin." Doug shook his head and laughed. "The Lost Boys."

"What do you mean by that?" I asked. But before he could answer, his phone rang.

"Hey, Gram! Yeah, I'm here with Arcade and Zoe . . . just passed the subway . . . What? . . . Whoops! Guess I forgot! Okay, I'll head back . . ." Doug hung up and then swallowed the last bite of his donut. "I forgot, I have an orthodontist appointment. Gotta run!" And that's exactly what he did, ran back toward the subway entrance.

"He's gonna have nasty donut in his teeth when he gets there."

"Yucko," Zoe said, and she began to walk toward home. "Let's change the subject. Did you meet any interesting people at school today?" She moved her eyebrows up and down.

"Yep. The Tolleys. They have this dent in their hair, and I'm trying to figure out how they got it." I put my hand on my head where their dents are and pushed down.

Zoe reached over with both hands and shoved me. "Not them. I'm asking if you met anyone cute. And nice. You know . . . like maybe a girl."

My face heated up, and I suddenly felt like I was going to puke. "No, I did *not*. And now *I'd* like to change the subject."

Zoe did a little quick-skip. "Okay, good, then let's talk about your necklace with the little gold medallion. I saw you try to hide it from me this morning. You owe me the story, remember?"

My sister is annoyingly smart. She totally set me up.

I sighed loud. "All right. I'll tell you. This little old lady gave it to me at the library."

"Was it the librarian?'

"No! Ms. Weckles is young."

"Then who was it? You know you shouldn't accept gifts from strangers."

"I don't know who she was. She just showed up, asked me if my name was Arcade and if I liked books, and then she slipped this around my neck. I called after her so I could give it back, but she disappeared."

"That's . . . weird."

I felt the token under my shirt heating up a little. "So what's new? *Everything* about life is weird lately. Dad wasn't kidding when he said to hold on. Don't you feel like you've been jerked around a lot? It really *is* like riding a bull in the rodeo. One minute we're in Virginia, then WHAM, we're in New York, with new schools, new friends, and who knows where we're gonna land? And have you noticed there's hardly any grass in our neighborhood?"

"There's tons of grass in Central Park."

"Yes, and *that* doesn't make sense either. We've got one huge park. For everyone in New York City."

I stopped and turned toward Zoe. Her face was lit up like someone was shining a flashlight on her. "Arcaaaaaaade . . ." Zoe pointed to the token.

"What?" I looked down at the glowing light on the end of the chain. I grabbed it. "It's been heating up all day. See? My life is crazy now. It doesn't make sense!"

And then the glitter fell.

CHAPTER 4

Hold On

It was like a zipper pouch opened above us, and silver-and-gold glitter poured down. It fell on Zoe's shiny black hair, making her look like an angel in a Christmas play.

"WHAT . . . IS . . . THIS . . . ?" Zoe danced around, shaking glitter off her head.

I laughed, though my heart was beating out of my chest. "I TOLD you New York was weird!" I glanced around, but no one else seemed to notice the change in the weather.

"Arcade, this has *nothing* to do with New York. It's *you*! You're making something happen with that token."

"WHAT? What am I making happen?"

And then doors appeared. Elevator doors, just like the ones in all the New York skyscrapers. But these doors had a shiny golden coin slot right in the middle. Light pulsed from the slot into my eyes. But it didn't blind me, it just made me curious. And New Yorkers all around us just pushed by on both sides of us, like nothing was there!

"Uh . . . Zoe? I think I'm supposed to put the token in there."

Zoe put her arm out in front of me. "Oh no you don't! I won't let you."

"But look!" I pointed to the token that was now pulsing its own light toward the coin slot.

Zoe turned and put her whole body in between me and the doors. She looked me square in the eyes. "Let's turn around and walk away." The glitter was still falling, and it had now coated her eyelashes.

I reached for the token, and it came off the chain and into my hand!

Zoe grabbed her throat and gasped. "Arcade, let's turn around and RUN away!"

"I can't Zoe, I think I have to do this. Check this out . . ." I turned the token over and showed her the words.

Arcade Adventures.

Zoe stared down at the pulsing token, her cheeks now covered in a glittery sheen. She moved to my left, facing the doors. She linked her right arm with my left arm and pulled me close to her side. "Whatever happens, I'll be right here with you."

I gulped and reached forward. My hand shook. It was so sweaty I thought I would drop the token. But no, it practically glided out of my hand into the slot.

The glitter stopped falling. Everything was dead silent. We just stared at the doors.

"Okay, open!" I yelled, making a parting motion with my hands. They opened.

"Wait!" Zoe yelled.

I tried to move, but she tightened her grip on my arm.

"We don't know what's in there!"

"Well, if we stay here, we'll never find out." I tugged my arm loose and stepped forward. "I'm going."

"No, you're not!"

"Yes, I am!"

Zoe grabbed my hood. "Not without me!"

I'm sitting on a bull. A real bull!

OH NO! I'M SITTING ON A BULL!

And he's NOT happy!

"This here's the wildest one we got, but you can handle him, Arcade. You're gonna win you some money today!"

The encouragement from the unknown cowboy sitting next to me on the rodeo gate is no comfort at all.

***WHAT** am I doing here?*

I reach up and feel the brim of a cowboy hat on my head. I've never in my whole life worn a cowboy hat. And on my legs . . . are those chaps? Weird, but cool. I wonder how I look? I crane my neck, searching for mirrors, but all I can see are hundreds of . . . rodeo fans?

I'll tell you how I look. I look SCARED.

"AND OVER IN GATE 23," an announcer who sounds like Mr. Dooley yells over the loudspeaker, "we have an epic matchup. Circuit Champ Arcade Livingston is preparing to ride Bone Crusher! No one's been able to tame this wild bull yet. We're in for a battle, ladies and gents! Stay tuned! We open the gate in sixty seconds!"

Sixty seconds? As in *one minute?*

Bone Crusher snorts and jerks me around inside the gate.

"Hey, guys! This is some kind of mistake! You gotta let me off this thing!"

Another cowboy laughs. "Arcade, you're a hoot! You got this!"

Cowboy number one spits in the ring. "Yeah, Arcade. You gotta show him who's boss!"

"Arcaaaade! I'm over here!"

I scan the bull-riding ring, and I spot her. Zoe. She's dressed as a rodeo clown. Her red nose has silver-and-gold sparkles on it. She's crouched down, like an outfielder at a baseball game, looking like she's ready to run left, maybe right . . .

"Zoe! I don't know how to ride a bull! You gotta get me outta here!"

The cowboy sitting next to me on the gate grabs me by the shoulders and squeezes. "Ha! That's what they all say sixty seconds before they ride. Don't worry, partner, it's just like riding a bike. You never forget how."

I have never ridden a bike like *this*. Smelly, huge, angry. With horns on its head! Horns that could be sticking me in the gut in sixty seconds!

"Arcade! I'm here to protect you!" Zoe comes in a little closer. "When you fall off, run away as fast as you can. I'll take care of Bone Crusher."

When I fall off? No, I WON'T be falling off, because I'm going back through those elevator doors right now.

I glance down at my chest. I push my free hand between the buttons of my plaid shirt and fumble around for it. But the token isn't there.

"And remember what Dad said!" Zoe is waving her arms like a mad woman.

"DAD? Is he *here*?"

The announcer comes back on. "Heeeeeere we go! In three, two, one . . . hold on, and enjoy the ride, Arcade!"

"Oh no . . . no, no, no, no, NOOOOOOOOOO! Zoooooooeeeeeeeeeee!"

A bell rings and metal clanks as the gate chute opens. Bone Crusher bucks backwards, and I turn into a human slinky. I feel my head hit Bone Crusher's backside.

That's gonna leave a mark.

"Hang on!" Zoe yells. And I think of Dad's note.

Hang on and enjoy the ride.

I'm hanging on, but I am NOT enjoying being flipped around and punched like pizza dough, even though hundreds of fans are cheering for me. And if I remember from the rodeo book I read, I have to endure this torture for something like EIGHT seconds.

I won't survive eight seconds!

Bone Crusher kicks up his hind legs, and my chin hits the back of his head. Now I'll have a bruise to match the one on my nose. It's a MIRACLE this cowboy hat is staying on!

"Make it stop! Make it STOP!" I yell. "AHHHHHHHHHHHHHHHHH!"

Bone Crusher flips me side-to-side. My neck cracks. I can't feel the fingers of my right hand, which is wedged under a rope that is tied around this mad bull. I imagine my whole body flying off, but my hand is staying there, under the rope. Chilling.

Five more seconds . . .

"Arcade! Arcade! Arcade!" The crowd roars.

Bone Crusher stops for a second. My vision focuses on Zoe, who is right in front of us. She puts her thumbs in her ears and waves at Bone Crusher. He takes off after her. My head hits his rear again.

"ZOOOOOOOOOEEEEEEEEE! Watch out for the horns!"

Four seconds . . .

Zoe turns and runs for a barrel. Bone Crusher is just one angry stomp behind her. She jumps, lands inside, and pulls her head in at the last minute. Bone Crusher hits the barrel full force with his horns, knocking it over, sending it rolling wildly around the ring.

The whole scene blurs as tears fly out of my eyes. I choke on the rising dust kicked up by Bone Crusher's fury. The only thing keeping me on is the fear of falling off.

Three seconds . . .

Zoe emerges from the barrel . . .

Thank you, God!

. . . and Bone Crusher sees her.

OH NO!

He snorts and bucks me around some more before taking off after her again. This time there's no barrel to hide in.

"I'm sorry, Zoe! I should have listened to you . . ."

"Arcade! Arcade! Arcade!" The crowd is ecstatic.

Two seconds . . .

Zoe turns, her ponytail whipping, and runs for the metal fence. I don't think she can jump that high.

God, please help her!

Bone Crusher snorts, rears back, and charges. Boy, can this huge bull run. He dips his head, the horns just inches from Zoe's back.

"JUMP, Zoe!"

And she does. Bone Crusher stops on a dime, launching me off his back, with my hand intact! Everything turns to slo-mo as I soar into the stratosphere. I start to close my eyes and brace for impact but falling glitter and a pulsing light from my chest catches my eye.

The token is back! And instead of hurtling into the stands, I'm now flying headfirst into elevator doors.

I reach for the token, it comes off in my hands, and just before I crash, I drop it into the golden slot.

"Arcade! Are you okay?" Zoe and I stood side-by-side, arms linked, exactly where we first saw the glitter falling by the subway entrance. We looked at each other with glazed eyes, and then collapsed on the ground, both of us crying, laughing, spitting, coughing, and breathing hard. A few people walked by us, staring, but not concerned.

I checked myself for broken bones. Everything felt like it was in place.

Did I just dream that? Am I about to drop another book on my face?

"Arc-a-ade, w-what just h-happened?" Zoe stood up and began brushing dirt off her jeans.

"I . . . have no idea. But I think we were just at a rodeo, I was riding a bull, and you were the rodeo clown."

Zoe grabbed her head with her hands. "No. That's impossible! We must be dehydrated, or sick, or daydreaming, or . . ."

Zoe walked around me in a circle. She put her hands out, forming the shape of elevator doors. Then she reached out, like she was feeling for something hidden in the air. "This *has* to be some kind of joke." She wrung her hands. "A hologram . . . *not* reality."

And then I spotted it. A red thing shoved inside the water-bottle netting on the side of Zoe's backpack.

I stood up and inched closer to look. It was her clown nose!

"Wow! That's dope!" I reached in for it and held it out to her. It still had some silver and gold glitter stuck to it. "It *was* real. I don't know how, and I don't know why, but it was real."

Zoe grabbed the nose from me. "I outsmarted that bull, didn't I?" One side of her mouth turned up in a grin.

I blew out my breath. "Whew. Yeah. Thanks for protecting me."

She pushed me in the chest, squishing the clown nose against my token. "You're welcome. It's what big sisters are supposed to do. But you better listen to me next time!"

We turned and began to walk toward home.

"So I guess my life isn't *exactly* like riding a bull at a rodeo. That, whatever it was, was too terrifying."

Zoe laughed. "I totally agree."

"But I am out of my comfort zone, that's for sure."

Zoe put a hand on my shoulder. "It'll be okay, Arcade. You'll see. And don't forget, we're in this together."

Chapter 5
How Was Your Day?

Dinner with my parents that night was . . . interesting.

"So, how was your day?" Mom asked. She *always* asks. "I am so sorry I couldn't be here this morning to kiss you both goodbye."

Mom is an adjunct professor at the local college. Adjunct means that she's not officially on the faculty, but she's so smart and talented that they hired her to be available to teach special courses as needed. Zoe's like my mom. Smart *and* overprotective of me.

And at this point in the conversation, Zoe was doing her job—protecting our secret by not letting me talk.

"It was a glorious day," Zoe gushed. "My new high school is *magnifique!* And I met some very nice new friends. Well, I don't know who my close friends will be yet, but there are definite possibilities. Let's see, there's Brooke, whose mom also works on Broadway. Taylor, who can speak two foreign languages—French and German! And Trista, who seriously sings like an angel . . . and, um, well, there was Michael Tolley. He was very helpful to me when

I arrived. For some reason, I couldn't find my first class, but Michael appeared out of the blue and walked me right where I needed to go."

Right out of the blue to help the beautiful new girl. What a gentleman!

Zoe went on. "And my teachers all seem so interested in helping the students succeed. My French teacher, Mademoiselle Sawyer, already thinks I should major in French in college . . ."

"Baaaaaak! Take a breath! Take a breath!"

That was Milo, Zoe's cockatoo. Zoe taught him how to talk, so it's like having an annoying kid brother in the house.

Everyone at the table busted out laughing. And I might have spit out a pea or two.

Zoe rolled her eyes. "I can't believe you taught him to say that, Arcade."

I pointed at myself in disbelief. "I didn't teach him, I said it ONCE. Like a year ago! He just learned it."

"Your bird's got spunk, Zoe," Dad said. "We should try him out for a part on Broadway."

"So how is your job going, Dad?" Zoe kicked me under the table, and then she twirled her index finger around in a circle as if to say, "Keep the dialogue going . . . anywhere but in your direction."

I cleared my throat. "Yeah, how is the stage working for the new show?"

Dad leaned to the side a little and rested his cheek in one hand. "It's great, son. The design team did a fine job, and the crew is quite competent at changing out the sets between acts. I'm pleased with the way things are turning out."

I smiled. "That's good. That's really, really good."

Zoe kicked me again.

"And how are the actors? Is the show getting good reviews?" I didn't know any more questions to ask about Broadway, since I'm a Virginia kid.

Dad put his fork down and relaxed back in his chair. "The reviews are good. You know the name of the show, right, Arcade?"

Gulp. Zooooooeeeeee. Help.

"*Manhattan Doors.* An intriguing title. I can't wait to see it, Dad."

Whew, my sister to the rescue. Again.

Mom reached over and tapped me on the hand. "I want to hear how *your* day went, Arcade." Uh-oh. She can *always* tell when I'm holding back information. It's best not to make eye contact.

"Well, it started with me dropping a large book on my face."

She peeked over the top of her glasses at me. "Reading in bed again?"

"Uh-huh."

She reached for her drink glass. "Well, that's fine with me, as long as you don't end up with a concussion." She took a sip of lemonade. "How was school?"

"Did you get my note?" Dad interrupted.

Okay, here goes. Answer him straight and get it over with.

"Yeah, I did. And you were right about hanging on, Dad. Being in a new school is a crazy ride. I don't know if I'm enjoying it just yet."

"But you didn't have any bone crushing defeats, right?"

My sister began to choke on her lemonade.

"Bone crushing! Bone crushing!" Birds are annoying creatures.

"No. See?" I held up my arms and twisted them around. "All in one piece." I turned to my sister. "Ever think of trading Milo in for a hamster?"

"How about friends? Did you meet any new friends?" Mom was not going to give up till I gave her some real answers.

"Ummm, I met some . . . people. Well, you know Doug, he was already my friend. He and couple of girls, Amber and Bailey, ended up on a team project with me. And there's this big, funny guy who scratches all the time who seems interesting. I'll probably try to talk to him on Monday."

Mom sighed. "Well, good. That all sounds promising. Not bad for starting at a new school at the end of March."

"You got the hardest day out of the way." Dad gave me a quick pat on the shoulder. "Good job, Arcade. It should be a breeze from here." He got up and wiped his mouth with a napkin. "Sorry, family, I gotta go. Tonight's show is a packed house."

I HATE that Dad has to work on Friday nights now. I know he loves what he's doing, but we used to get pizza, play football outside till dark, and then watch movies together as a family on Fridays.

This new schedule just doesn't make sense.

As soon as that thought came into my brain, my pocket heated up where I was hiding my chain with the token.

Mom leaned back in her chair. "Okay, whose turn is it to do the dishes?"

"Mine!" Zoe and I yelled at the same time.

Chapter 6
Token Secrets

Zoe rinsed, and I loaded the dishwasher. And we only talked when the water was going full blast, so no one could hear—especially Milo.

"Arcade, you *have* to find that old lady and give her the token back."

"Why?"

"Why? *Why*? Because we almost got killed by a bull today, that's why."

"But we didn't." I pointed to my chin. "And look, no bruise! How did that happen?"

Zoe kept the water on but stopped rinsing to face me. "Oh, sure, you're sounding all brave now. But you were screaming and crying like a baby, and you know it."

"Okay, yeah. I was freaking out. But now that I look back on it, it wasn't so bad."

"Oh, *s'il te plaît*!" Zoe grabbed me by the elbow and wouldn't let go until she had escorted me upstairs, into my room. "This is serious business, Arcade! I don't know what's going on, but we have to get a handle on it. Can I see the token?" She held out her hand, waiting for me to just drop it right in.

Instead, I took it out of my pocket, put it around my neck, and let her hold it as it dangled from the chain.

She examined the front of it carefully. "What do you suppose the three Ts connected together mean?"

I pulled back and let out a nervous laugh. "I dunno. Totally Terrific Treasure?"

She let go of the token and frowned. "Or it could mean Transport to Trouble."

"Ah, Zoe. I can't believe that."

"Well, how do you explain today? We *were* transported to trouble! Arcade, you have to *promise* me that you won't use that thing to go anywhere without me." She shook her index finger. I *hate* when she does that.

"Use it? I don't even know how it works! I'm still not even sure what happened."

"Then leave it here. Hide it." Zoe walked over to my dresser, opened the top drawer, and looked in. "Dude, you should fold your underwear."

I ran over to the drawer and shoved it closed. "Hey— don't judge. I have a system."

She giggled. "Okay, sorry. But whatever you do, *don't* take that thing to school with you again." Zoe paced the room. She started thinking out loud, going back and forth between French and English. "Arcade, did the old woman *say* anything to you after she gave you the token?"

I moved a few books over so I could sit down on my bed. "Yeah, she said two words."

Zoe plunked down next to me. "What did she say?"

"She said, 'Happy travels.'"

"Happy?"

"Yeah, happy. So that's why we gotta go again."

"Go where?"

"Wherever this little token takes us."

CHAPTER 7
Weekend Welcome

First thing Saturday morning, I got a call from my cousin, Derek.

"Hey, Arcade! When you movin' back to Virginia?"

"Very funny, Derek."

My cousin is the same age as me, and we've been best friends pretty much since birth. And that's another reason why I hated this move to New York. Derek and I used to hang out constantly. But now, we just call and once-in-a-while do a face chat.

"I can't hang with the idea that you won't be comin' to my basketball games this season. You're my best cheerleader."

Derek is right. I jump up and down, make a bunch of goofy noises, and throw my hands in the air. Like I just don't care.

"I know. I'm sorry."

"So, did you go and get some new friends to hang with and forget about me?"

"Nah, I'd never do that!"

"Then what are you gonna do today?"

"Goin' to the library. I had to leave twenty-three books there because now we walk and take the subway instead of using a car, and I couldn't carry them all. So I have to go visit them."

And I'm hoping to see a little old lady about a mysterious token.

Derek laughed. "Man, you gotta get yourself a rolling suitcase! Anyway, I'm glad you're still learning all kinds of stuff. You're gonna have to tutor me so I can get into college."

"Dude, you gotta pass the sixth grade first."

"Hey, it could happen! I only got a few weeks left. And I moved my D average up to a C minus."

"You know if you started doin' all your homework that would help."

"But it's not fun without you!"

"Well, just *try*. And, hey, Derek, I have a question . . ."

"Is this about the stop sign again?"

"Not this time. It has to do with a big project we're working on at school."

"Oh, cool. I get to help *you* with school for a change?"

"Yeah. Do you know what you want to be when you grow up?"

"Aw, man, that's easy. NBA point-guard."

"Anything else?"

"Huh. I dunno. Maybe a vet. I like animals."

Something in the medical field. That would work!

"Hey, Derek, can I call you back later?"

"Oh, so you gonna go hang out with all your new friends now?"

"Nah. I told you I'm going to the library. To work on the project. You just gave me an idea."

"Okay, then. But call me later, okay?"

"I will."

"Okay. Later, dude."

"Later."

A veterinarian. That would be a good thing to be. Then, if Loopy ever got sick, I could fix him.

I threw on my weekend clothes—basketball shorts and a tank top—but then I changed my mind and put on a T-shirt with a high collar so I could hide Triple T. I ran downstairs, where Mom and Zoe were having scones for breakfast.

"Well, look at you, all bright-eyed and prickly, like a cute little pufferfish." Zoe puffed out her cheeks, but I could see her eyes searching my neck for the token and chain.

"Mom, can I go to the library?"

Mom wiped a few scone crumbs from her lips with a napkin. "The library doesn't open till ten o'clock. Did you already read the three books you checked out last time?"

I approached the kitchen table and grabbed a scone. "Almost, and if you could lend me a rolling suitcase, this time I can bring a bunch more home on the subway."

Mom leaned back and sighed. "I'm glad you like reading, Arcade. But, really, a suitcase?"

"I think it's a pretty clever idea," Zoe said. "And I'll go with him if it's okay with you, Mom. I have some studying to do myself." Zoe glanced over at me and raised an eyebrow.

No, she doesn't. She wants to find the lady who gave me the token.

Mom checked her watch.

"Well, I've got some work to do, and your father won't be up for a few hours, so it's okay with me. By the time you get there, they'll almost be open."

"Awesome! Thanks, Mom. Do you have that suitcase?"

I was almost sorry I asked when she returned from the upstairs storage closet wheeling a lime green suitcase with white daisies all over it.

"WHAT IS THAT?" I guess I was expecting a black one, like *everyone* else has.

Zoe grabbed her belly and bent over, laughing. "That's perfect!"

I squinted at the sight of the bright suitcase. "Are you sure this is the only one you've got?"

Mom put her hand over her mouth, but I could see her big smile. "No, but the others are in the bedroom closet with clothes in them that still need to be unpacked. I don't want to wake up your father, so if you want all those books today, you'll have to go with this one."

I turned to Zoe. "Do *you* have a rolling suitcase I can borrow?"

She laughed some more. "You want mine with the mermaids all over it?"

I reached out and grabbed the suitcase handle. "Daisies it is."

We finished up our scones, Zoe got dressed, and we headed out toward the subway to go to the library.

And, of course, *this* was the first day I ran into the Tolleys in the neighborhood.

"Hey—look! It's that Arcade kid! Hey, Arcade!"

The Tolleys were hanging out on the bottom step of an apartment just three doors down and across the street.

Please, God, don't let them live there. That's tooooo close.

A nicely-groomed older boy stood a couple of steps up from the Tolleys, leaning on the railing. He spotted us and came jogging over to . . . Zoe.

"Hi, Zoe. I didn't know you lived right here."

Zoe pushed some of her long black hair behind one ear.

"Yes, this is my house. And this is my little brother, Arcade."

The boy reached his hand out to shake mine.

"Hello, Arcade. I'm Michael Tolley."

He didn't look at all like the other two Tolleys. I tried to keep from staring. He didn't have a wrinkle anywhere on his clothes. And he was wearing a polo shirt and dress shorts on a Saturday.

"Hey, Arcaaaaade! Your parents kick you outta the house? Nice suitcase!"

I glanced over to see one of the Tolley twins throw a basketball up in the air, grab it, and then spin it around his thick waist a couple of times.

Michael turned. "Casey . . ."

That's all he said. Casey. And the Tolley brother with the basketball shut up and sat down.

"Don't worry about my brothers," Michael said. "They have yet to learn how to properly greet new people to the neighborhood." Then he looked a little closer at the suitcase. "Just curious, where are you two going with such a . . . cheery suitcase?"

Zoe grinned. "Library. My brother and I like books, and we're going to use that to carry them home."

Michael crossed his arms and put one hand up to his chin. "That's genius. I've often found myself with the same problem. I'm going to try it next time I go to the library."

"Would you like to join us today?" Zoe asked. But then she shot me a funny glance, like, *Oops, maybe I shouldn't have asked.*

"I'd like to," Michael said. "But I'm waiting for a ride to take me to my voice lesson. That's why I'm dressed up a little."

"You sing?" I couldn't shake the shock that this boy was related to the other Tolleys.

"Yes, I sing tenor in the choir. I'm getting a little extra training from Trista's mom. She's an opera singer."

"Trista?" Zoe's eyes widened. "I met a Trista at school yesterday."

Right then, a car rolled down the street, and a girl with long, black curly hair reached out the back window and waved. “Hey, Michael! Ready to go? Hey, Zoe! Great to see you!”

Both Michael and Zoe waved to the girl.

“Yep, that’s her,” Michael said. “Trista’s my girlfriend. We’re working on a duet together to sing at the choir festival next month.”

Zoe kept her smile, but now it looked forced. She took a couple of steps back. “Well, we better be going. I hope you have a good practice.”

Michael smiled back at Zoe. “And I hope you fill that suitcase full of interesting books. I’d like to see them later on.” Then he ran into the street, jumped in the backseat with Trista, and the car sped off.

Zoe grabbed the suitcase handle. “Let’s get out of here,” she said, taking long strides.

“Have a nice vacation!” one of the Tolley brothers yelled, and then they both laughed.

“Zoe, wait up! Why are you walking so fast?” I was out of breath and I hadn’t even rounded the second corner yet.

Zoe kept her eyes on the sidewalk. “Time is precious, Arcade. Don’t you want to be there right when they open?”

I pushed my glasses up onto the sweaty bridge of my nose. “Well, yeah. But, it’s only 9:15, and if you keep up this cheetah pace, we’re gonna be early.”

Zoe stopped and frowned. She reached for the back of my neck and pinched the token chain between her fingers. "You were supposed to leave *this* in your systematic underwear drawer, remember?"

"But if we see the lady at the library, we can ask her about it."

Zoe sighed loudly. "Okay, then. Let's go." She took off again, and I struggled to keep up.

"Hey, how come you're grouchy all of a sudden?"

"I'm not grouchy, Arcade. And you wouldn't understand if I told you."

"You got that right. Older sisters don't make a lot of sense." The token under my shirt heated up just then.

"And neither do little brothers. But we're *all* we've got in this crazy new town, so we'll have to make the best of it."

We reached the subway entrance, and Zoe walked around in a circle. "Do you think the doors are still here?"

I made the door-opening gesture with my hands. Nothing happened. "Maybe yesterday was just a dream." I squinted, hoping to see glitter in the distance, but there was none.

"Maybe this whole move to New York City is a *nightmare*," Zoe added. And with that, she dragged the bright, daisy-covered suitcase down the steps and into the subway.

CHAPTER 8

Tolley Triangle

There's nothing more exciting than standing at the doors of an about-to-open library. I always head for the "New Arrival" shelves first, so I can be the first person to crack open a book, sniff the paper-and-print aroma, and then check it out before anyone else has a chance.

"Where did you say you saw the lady?" Zoe asked as we passed by the circulation desk.

"She was in the kids' section. Travel." I pointed in the direction of Ms. Weckles' desk.

"Okay, I'm going over there." Zoe held out the suitcase handle, and I grabbed it from her.

"I want to check New Arrivals first, but I'll meet you there soon."

Zoe took off to the right and passed the aquarium that separates the kids' and adult sections. I stayed straight and wheeled the daisy suitcase over to see what new books would jump into it. *New York City: A Coffee Table Tour* was the first to catch my eye. I pulled it off the shelf. "Oof! You're heavy." I could bench press the book a few times a day and gain major muscle mass over the three-week check-out period.

I carried it over to one of the reading desks and thumped the book down. I pulled up a chair and sat down, opened the book to the center, put my nose in, and took a whiff. "Ahh, can't beat that." I whiffed again. "So tell me," I said to the book, "what's the big deal about New York?"

But before I could learn one single fact, someone big sat down next to me and interrupted my tour.

"Hey, Arcade," the huge mass whispered, "I thought I'd find you here."

It was a Tolley. And not the older, smarter one. But was it *only one*? I thought these scruffy guys came in a pair.

I tried to appear friendly and flashed a grin. "Hello."

The Tolley placed his elbow on the table and rested his head in his hand. "Hey, I need help, and you're the smartest dude in our class."

"How do you know that? You just met me."

Tolley looked around. "You're *here*, right? Smart people hang out at libraries. Plus, I can just tell."

"But *you're* here too," I replied, hoping compliments kept Tolleys nice and calm.

"Only 'cause I followed *you*." Tolley pushed me in the shoulder. "And I had to ditch Casey, which wasn't easy."

So this one was Kevin. "How can I help you, Kevin?"

He put his hand on the back of my neck and squeezed. "Well, you see Arcade, I don't know what to do for my class project. I don't know what jobs are out there, and I don't know how to pick one to do a display on."

Okay. Maybe I could help with this. I leaned away from Kevin, which loosened his gorilla grip on my neck.

"Well, you've come to the right place." I put my hand up and swept it around the library. "We can talk to Ms. Weckles, and she can help you find anythi—"

Kevin grabbed my wrist. "You don't understand. I need you to *do* the project for me. And, I want it to be the *best one* in the class, so my team will win. In exchange for your hard work, I'll make sure no ugly rumors get started about you at school."

I grimaced. "Who would start ugly rumors about me?"

"Yeah, who would do a terrible thing like that?" He laughed through a sinister grin.

Great.

"So," Kevin continued, "it looks like we have a deal. You know the first part of the project is due in two weeks. I'll need my job title, education, special training requirements, and a rough sketch of my amazing display. You got that?"

I shook my head. "But I have my own project to do . . ."

Kevin slapped his hand down hard on the table, and several library patrons shushed him. "So you better get started." Then he got up and walked out of the library like he didn't have a care in the world.

I, on the other hand, now had a major problem. My

mind began playing out different scenarios. I *could* do two projects, but I also wanted a life. And what kind of job could a big, mean guy like Kevin Tolley be good at anyway? I ticked through the possibilities.

Linebacker. Dog Catcher. Bouncer.

I was hitting a dead end.

How bad of a rumor could he start about me, anyway?

"Arcade . . ."

I jumped a mile.

Zoe put her hands up and stepped back. "Sorry! I didn't mean to scare you. I didn't see a little old lady anywhere near the travel section. But I did find a French cookbook, and now I'm going to go check the adult travel section."

"O . . . kay."

"Hey, what's the matter?"

I glanced over at the library entrance. Thankfully, Kevin Tolley was long gone. "Nothing. I'm fine. I found this huge book about New York City. Maybe it will tell me why we only have one park."

Zoe rolled her eyes and knocked on my head. "Hello. We have more than one park, Arcade. Central Park is just the biggest one."

I laid the suitcase down on the floor and unzipped it. "Well, good. I'll find out all about it, because I'm checking this one out."

Zoe placed her French cookbook on top of the New York book.

I zipped up the suitcase. "I'm going to go read in the kids' section. I'll meet you over there."

Zoe helped me lift the suitcase to the standing position. "Try not to overload and break this thing on its first trip to the library. That New York book must weigh fifty pounds."

I wheeled "Daisy" over to my favorite reading spot in the kids' section—a couch that's almost hidden in a wall by the computers. I can usually fit myself and a stack of books right next to me. But as I approached, I saw that there would be no room for books.

Kevin Tolley had returned, and he was sitting on *my* couch! "Hey, Arcade, I thought I might find you here. Doug said you were a bookworm." He gestured to me to come sit down next to him.

I gulped.

He started laughing. "That suitcase. Dude! Couldn't you have picked one with dragons on it or something tough like that?"

"It's my mom's," I said, and I wedged myself into the tight spot left on the couch.

He whispered in my ear, "I ditched Kevin so I could find you and tell you something really important. But you have to promise not to tell him anything about this talk, okay?"

Oh, no. This is Casey!

Casey rested his elbow on my shoulder, and the odor from his armpit nearly knocked me over. "You and I are going to be secret partners on this sixth-grade project. I know we're not on the same team, but we can still work together, right? I'm a great builder, so this is what I figure. You can do *all* the research and writing for me, and I'll build whatever you come up with for my display."

So at least Casey was a twin with a talent.

I told him the same thing I tried to tell Kevin. "But, I already have my own project to do . . ."

Casey flicked my glasses, making them sit crooked on my face. "Yeah, but you're smart. You'll have time for two. And, oh yeah, I want mine to be the best so that my team wins. And in exchange for all your hard work, I'll make sure none of your stuff gets ripped off at school."

"Who's gonna rip my stuff off at school?"

Casey shrugged. "I know, right?"

I mentally ticked off possible jobs for Casey.

Spy. Demolitionist. Deodorant tester.

"I think we've got some stuff due in a couple of weeks. Just pick me a job and write up how much school I need for it. I'll build a 3D model of the display that you design. That oughta get me a good grade on the first part." Casey gave me a noogie, and then stood up next to my suitcase. "Got that?"

"Got it," I said with a heavy sigh.

"I better go. I'm sure Kevin's out lookin' for me. Hey, at least I know he'd never come in here." And then Casey Tolley ran out of the library.

I stood and walked in a daze to the only person I knew who could help me in a moment like this. Ms. Weckles.

"Well, hello, Arcade. How are you doing today? I heard you're attending PS 23! I work there part-time, you know. Is that your suitcase?" She pointed over to Daisy in the corner by the couch.

I nodded. "Well, yes, I'm using it. It's my mom's. I need

to fill it with books about jobs. As *many* jobs as possible, please. I have some big year-end projects to finish. I mean one year-end project. They—I mean, *it*—has to do with what I want to be when I grow up."

Ms. Weckles cracked a huge smile. "You should be a librarian when you grow up, Arcade. Then you can hang out with all these books, all the time! And you can help kids with projects."

"I like helping people."

But I don't like being bullied into it.

Ms. Weckles checked a couple things on her computer and then got up from her desk.

"So let's see about those books. Follow me over to the career section. And bring your suitcase."

Ms. Weckles to the rescue! With her on my side, maybe, just maybe, there was hope for me and the Tolley brothers.

CHAPTER 9

Monday Morning Madness

I read up on jobs all weekend, and I put together two lists—one for Team One and a secret list for the Tolleys. And today I had a mission: decide by the end of the day if I was going to do their projects *for* them, or risk having ugly rumors spread about me and all my stuff ripped off.

Dad's morning note didn't help much with the decision.

> *Happy Monday, Arcade!*
> *Glad you are meeting new people. Always remember, when choosing who to hang out with:*
>
> *As iron sharpens iron, so a friend sharpens a friend.*
> — PROVERBS 27:17 (NLT) —
>
> *Love, Dad*

I had read that Bible verse before, and I agreed with the wisdom. Friends help friends become better people. So, how would I find friends like that here in New York? Especially when I was being FORCED to hang out with the Tolley twins?

"Zoe, what does *your* note say?"

I didn't even wait for her to read it to me. I just snatched it off the table and read it aloud.

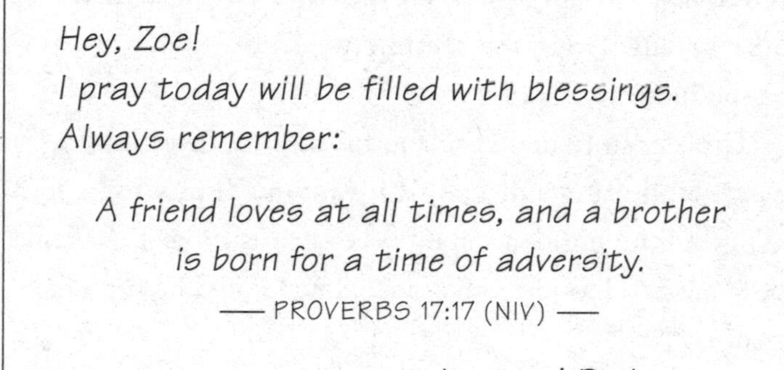

Hey, Zoe!
I pray today will be filled with blessings.
Always remember:

A friend loves at all times, and a brother is born for a time of adversity.

— PROVERBS 17:17 (NIV) —

Love ya! Dad

"Bawwwwk! Adversity!"

"Milo, you don't even know what adversity means." I scratched my head. "I'm not sure I do either."

Zoe came over and showed me her phone screen. She had pulled up an online dictionary, because, of course, *her* phone doesn't have any restrictions.

"The definition of adversity: Difficulties, trouble, hardship. See, I told you, fish breath, we've got to stick together."

"Zoe, what's wrong with your knee?"

She looked down. "Nothing's wrong with my knee."

I lifted my big New York book from the coffee table and pushed it into the back of her leg, right where the knee bends. Her knee gave out, and she had to catch herself so she wouldn't tumble onto the floor. It was hilarious.

"A brother *is* adversity," she snarled, and she chased me out the door and down the steps of our brownstone, where Doug sat waiting to walk to school with us.

On the way to the subway, I wondered if I should tell Zoe about the Tolleys and their threats. But I never had the chance because Doug was talking my ear off about careers in the food industry.

"Grocery store manager, food inspector, nutritionist . . . the possibilities are endless! But I want my display to be fun! So I'm thinkin' hot dog stand owner or pastry chef. I wanna have some good food to give out. Hey, I could be the cake boss of PS 23!"

"Doug, do you even know how to bake a cake?"

He looked at me funny. "Do I know how to bake a cake?"

"That's what I asked."

"Uh. No. But that's just details, right?"

"Details are important, Doug. Without them, nothing makes sense."

Right then, the token started to burn my chest.

"Ouch!" I grabbed the chain and pulled it out of the front of my shirt. "I'm getting real tired of this!" I said to no one in particular.

"What are you gettin' tired of?" Doug stepped in close to me and examined the token. It was flashing, making his eyes glow. "Nice! Did you get that in your cereal box this morning?"

"Oh no!" Zoe gasped and tightened her backpack straps. "We don't have time for this, Arcade. We have to get to school!" And then glitter dropped from the sky. Or at least it looked like glitter.

Doug looked up. "Are those *donut* sprinkles?" He stuck his tongue out and caught a few. "Whoa! They ARE sprinkles! Hey, is this some kind of TV prank? Are there cameras hiding somewhere?" Doug ran around a bit but found nothing but more sprinkles. "This is cool, man!"

Just like before, New Yorkers pushed by us, seemingly unaware of the falling, sugarcoated debris. And then the elevator doors appeared again, with the golden coin slot right in the middle.

Zoe put a hand on her cheek. "Keep walking, Arcade. I don't feel like clowning around today, if you know what I mean. You should have left that thing at home!"

Now Doug was staring at the coin slot. "This . . . did NOT come from any cereal box I've seen!" He reached his hand out to touch the doors. "WHERE DID THESE COME FROM? This is CRAZY!"

I scooted over near Zoe and whispered in her ear, "What do you suppose is behind the doors?"

"WHAT DO YOU SUPPOSE IS BEHIND THE DOORS?" Doug tried to pry them apart.

Zoe grabbed me by both my shoulders and glared into my eyes. "I don't know, and you DO NOT NEED TO FIND OUT."

My whole body broke out in goosebumps and my heart pounded in my chest. "Zoe, what if I *do* need to find out?

What if it's *happy travels*, like the lady said? What if it's better than going to PS 23 today?"

"Hey, Arcade." Doug gestured between the flashing coin slot and the pulsing token still hanging around my neck. "Do you think your fancy coin goes in this slot?" He shook sprinkles out of his shirt and then shrugged. "I say, give it a try, man!"

I held my hands up and looked at Zoe. "He says give it a try, man."

Zoe shook her index finger at me. "If you make me late for school, or if I miss school, or if you get hurt, or we end up lost somewhere. . . . Ugh! Arcade! You make me *so mad*!"

"It's gonna be okay, Zoe. You'll see." With that, I stepped forward. I pulled on the token, and it came off the chain right in my hand.

Doug hit his forehead with his palm. "WHOA. I don't know whether I should stay or run away!"

I slipped the coin into the slot and made an opening motion with my hands. The doors opened.

Doug hit his forehead again, this time with his other palm, a little too hard, maybe, because he stumbled backward. "MIND. BLOWN. But I'm STAYING!" Then he took a deep breath, looked both ways as if he were about to cross a busy street, and with a huge smile on his face, ran through the doors. "I hope there's food in here!"

I looked at Zoe. "Well, now we have to go after him."

Zoe rolled her eyes. "You have weird friends, Arcade."

We're in a television studio. I'm sure of it. Cameras are everywhere—lights too. Zoe and I sit in canvas chairs behind the cameras, looking at a set that has a long counter with some big bowls on it. Three people wearing chef hats sit on stools on the other side of the counter, facing us and the cameras.

Doug is one of those people.

At least I'm *pretty sure* it's Doug. He's got some new bushy eyebrows and long sideburns, and he's either a lot taller than he was a second ago, or he's sitting on a huge booster seat. He's munching down on something that looks like white clay.

Zoe gasps. "*Fou*! He's eating the fondant!"

"Huh? What's fondant?"

Zoe giggles. "It's special icing that's used for decorating cakes. It looks beautiful, but it tastes . . ." she twists up her face . . . "twangy."

Yep. That *has* to be Doug.

"Okay, Madison, whenever you're ready." A man sitting behind one of the cameras motions to a tall, dark-haired woman wearing a blue dress with a cooking apron over it. She glances over some papers, sets them down on a side table, and then walks over to the counter with Doug, the other two people, and the bowls. She smiles at the camera.

"Today on *The Munch*, we'll uncover secrets of some of New York's finest pastry chefs. They've each brought their favorite ingredients to create something decadent and beautiful by the end of our sixty minutes together. We'll meet them and discuss what makes a cake irresistible when we return."

"Time out!" Doug yells and makes a T with his hands. Then he jumps off his stool.

The guy behind the camera gets up and starts pacing around the room. I think Doug's appearance on *The Munch* may be short-lived.

Doug jets over to me and Zoe. "Check *these* out." He wiggles his eyebrows up and down and twists his thick sideburns between his fingers.

Zoe giggles some more. "They make you look sophisticated."

"Am I really on a TV show? About to make a cake?" Doug takes a bite of the white fondant that he still has in his hand. "What *is* this? It's *ridiculously* good."

Zoe pulls a small piece out of his hand, rolls it between her hands into a little ball, and holds it out for him to see. "It's called fondant, Doug. Used for decorating. It's edible, but it's not considered the best tasting part of the cake."

"It's not? Mmmmm. Then the rest of the cake must be FAAAANTASTIC."

People start moving all around us on the set as lights click on and off. The pacing guy yells out, "We're back in three minutes, people!"

"Excuse me, Mr. Baker?" The woman with the apron, Madison, taps Doug on the shoulder. "Are you ready to go? We've got all the ingredients for the recipe you gave us measured and in bowls. All you have to do is whip up your cake. After the next break, we'll bring out the finished product and you can decorate. I can't wait to watch a master at work!"

Doug just stands there, chewing fondant. "I gave you a recipe?"

Madison nods. "Yes. For your famous white chocolate raspberry wedding cake. Remember?"

Doug licks his lips and examines the ceiling for a second. Something changes in his expression. All of a sudden, he has his game face on. "Delicious white chocolate cake swirled with a smooth raspberry puree? Fluffy, moist, and so good you'll want it all to yourself?"

Madison raises up on her toes and points at Doug. "That's the one!"

Zoe pulls me aside and smacks me in the chest. "What is going *on* here?"

I pull on the empty chain around my neck. "Who knows? It sure seems like he knows what he's doing. Well, except for that fondant-eating part. It's pretty funny that his last name's Baker."

Doug overhears and puts a finger on his chin. "Hey, my name *is* Baker, isn't it? Guess I better go bake." He walks behind the counter with a huge grin on his face. "Let's go, people! White chocolate raspberry greatness awaits!"

The other two chefs join him on either side. Doug picks up a small, metal whisk and a bowl. He dips the whisk in, then tilts his head back. He lifts the whisk up, causing drips of red raspberry syrup to stream off it *into his mouth*.

I draw my fingers across my throat. "NO! Doug! You're on national TV!"

"This is going to be a disaster," Zoe says. "Worse than the rodeo!"

"Maybe. But maybe not. He seems to know the recipe."

"But he has no table manners! What's he going to do next, lick the beaters? We gotta get him out of there, Arcade."

The guy behind the camera starts giving directions. "Okay, Madison, whenever you're ready."

"I'm ready as I'll ever be." She steps behind the counter and squeezes in right next to Doug.

"In three . . . two . . . one . . . ACTION!"

Glitter and donut sprinkles fall from the ceiling. It's so thick I can barely see Doug. I reach for the chain, and there's the token. Now all we need are the elevator doors . . .

"Doug Baker, famous wedding cake chef from right here in New York City, is about to divulge the secret to his scrumptious white chocolate raspberry wedding cake . . ."

"And it's right here in this bowl," Doug says. He lifts the whisk again. Thankfully, the doors appear, just as the drips of raspberry are about to hit his tongue.

I make the parting motion, and they open.

"How are we going to get Doug over here?" Zoe grabs my hand, and she's shaking. "I told you this was going to be a disaster!"

"Zoe, stay calm. I know what to do."

I cup my hands to my mouth and scream . . .

"CANDY!"

"Candy?" I hear Doug say. And then he yells, "TIME OUT!"

He's next to us in within seconds. And we all run back through the doors together.

"What were you saying about not knowing how to bake a cake, Doug?" I chuckled and brushed donut sprinkles off my backpack.

Doug stared into space. I didn't blame him. The token had a way of doing that to people.

"Wha-???? Where??? How????"

Zoe looked down at her watch, astounded. "Good. No time has passed. But we still have to get a move on if we're going to make it to school without a tardy."

"Wha-??? Where??? How???"

Poor Doug. I grabbed him by the elbow and began moving him forward. "I'll explain everything I know—which isn't much—on the way to school." Then I laughed. "One thing I know *for sure.* You shouldn't consider being a pastry chef when you grow up."

Doug's phone buzzed and jolted him out of his trance. "It's a text from Bailey." He handed me the phone, like he just couldn't concentrate to read it.

"Planning meeting today at Ivy Park Park. Bring your dogs. We can walk them while we plan," I read out loud.

I scratched my head. "Is that a typo? Is there an Ivy Park *Park?"*

Zoe shoved her elbow in my side. "Told ya there are other parks."

I scrunched my face up. "But why do we have to say the word "Park" twice? Ivy Park Park?"

Zoe shook her head. "Oh, no, here we go. You ask *too many questions*."

"But it sounds ridiculous! Ivy Park Park? Hey, Doug, you wanna go to the Park Park?"

Doug still seem dazed but played along. "You wanna go to the Park Park? Yeah, I wanna go to the Park Park."

"You guys are gonna make me crazy. What time is this meeting at the Ivy Park . . . green space?"

"Says here four o'clock." I handed Doug's phone back to him.

"That doesn't leave you much time to get there, Arcade. I get out of school a little early today. Do you want me to bring Loopy and meet you over at the park?"

"Sure, thanks." Zoe wasn't going to let me out of her sight as long as the token was in the picture.

"Do you have a dog, Doug?" I tapped Doug on the arm to make sure he was still functioning.

"Nah." Doug's phone buzzed again. This time he read it himself. "Uh-oh. This just in! Gram says I'm getting my braces on today." He looked up at me, bleary-eyed. "Guess I'm gonna miss the meeting."

"Braces?" I hated to break it to him. "Isn't that going to cramp your food style?"

"What do you mean?" Doug grabbed his stomach like I had just punched him in the gut.

"When you wear braces, you can't eat certain kinds of foods."

His mouth dropped open. "WHAT? Like fondant?"

Zoe laughed and began ticking off a list. "Popcorn, some cheeses, sticky candy . . ."

"Sticky candy? Like Gummy Bears?" Doug looked horrified.

"Especially no Gummy Bears," Zoe said.

"Well, forget it then. I'm *not* getting braces. I'll find me a dog and join the meeting this afternoon."

"Then your teeth will turn out all snaggly, and you'll scare little kids," I said.

"Then I'm gonna invent new braces. Yep, that's what I'll do. Since I can't be a good pastry chef, I'll be an inventor. I'll invent Gummy Braces. Kids will love me."

As we approached the subway entrance, I looked up to see if there were glitter clouds in the sky.

Zoe must have read my mind, because she looked up too, and then she made that open-door gesture with her hands.

Nothing.

"Have a good day at school," Zoe said. "I'll bring Loopy to Ivy Park Park at four o'clock."

"Thanks, Zoe. And make sure you go to Ivy Park *Park*. Not Ivy Park. There's a difference, you know."

"I think your brain is in park." She flicked me on the side of my head and then disappeared down the steps.

"Hey, Arcade," Doug said. "Do you think any of the kids at school saw me on *The Munch*?"

"Ha! If they did, they wouldn't have recognized you. Sideburns, remember?"

Doug reached up and rubbed his face near his ear. "Oh, yeah. Sideburns. Those were cool. But this has been the strangest morning *ever.* Where'd you say you got that arcade token?"

I grinned. "The library."

"Man, all I ever got from the library was candy."

We talked about the token the rest of the way to school. There wasn't much to tell, but Doug promised to keep what we did know secret. He looked a little less dazed when we finally arrived at room 603, where a large greeter stood blocking the entrance to the classroom. It was a Tolley.

CHAPTER 10

Confusion, All Kinds

The Tolley brother let Doug through the door, but then put his arm out to block me from entering.

Doug looked back. "I wouldn't mess. That bookworm's got super powers."

DOUG!

Tolley scowled. "Come over here, Arcade." He moved toward the drinking fountain and bent over to take a drink. "So, did your 'super powers' help you find a good job for me yet?" Tolley slurped water, most of it dripping down his stained, white T-shirt.

Dry cleaner, maybe?

"Not yet, but I got a whole bunch of books at the library. You could come over to my house and choose . . ."

The Tolley brother stood up straight. "Nah. I'm not doing *any* of this, remember?"

"Not even building your display?"

He wiped his wet mouth with his sleeve. "Are you crazy? I don't build stuff."

Kevin.

"Uh, okay, then. I have some ideas in my backpack. Let me go get . . ."

The bell rang.

Mr. Dooley stuck his head out the door. "STUDENTS STILL OUTSIDE SHOULD BE INSIDE. DO YOU HEAR ME?"

The truth was, my cousin Derek all the way in Virginia could probably hear him, but I didn't dare say that. I hurried into the room and sat down. Next to Amber.

"Good morning," she said.

"Good boarding." Good *boarding*? *Really?* Ugh, nerves.

Amber giggled under her breath.

"TODAY, YOU WILL COME UP WITH TEAM NAMES SO I DON'T HAVE TO KEEP REFERRING TO YOU AS NUMBERS." Mr. Dooley had a megaphone for a Monday voice.

"Yes!" Doug pumped his fist. And he was the first to drag his chair over. "I think our name should be the Gummies." And then he popped a Gummy Bear in his mouth.

"Please," Bailey said. "Let's not go down this road of silliness." She bit down on her pencil. "I want people to take us seriously. How about a more professional name, like . . . the Career Council?"

Doug gave her a look like he just sucked on a lemon. "Oh no. Sounds too . . . too . . ."

"Collegiate, I know." Bailey shook her head and tapped her pencil on the desk. "And boring. I'm sorry, I withdraw that suggestion."

"You want to withdraw your boring suggestion?"

"Doug!" I shook my pencil at him. "No need to rub it in." For some reason, right at that moment, my token started heating up. I grabbed it, and that gave me an idea. "Hey. How about Triple T?"

"Triple T?" Bailey tapped her pencil some more. "Team Triple T? That's catchy. But what in the world does Triple T mean?"

You tell me. Could be anything. Transport to trouble . . .

"Totally Terrific Team," Amber said. "I like it."

"Because that's what we are!" Doug stood up and held his hands in the air like a rock star. "Triple T it is!"

"Don't you think we should vote on it first?" Bailey had finally put her pencil down and was leaning back in her chair.

I stood. "Everyone who would like our name to be Team Triple T . . . fist-bump Doug." I was the first one to do it. Then Amber did. Finally, Bailey stood, pushed her chair back, and held out a fist.

"Okay, then. Team Triple T—the best career team in the class!" Bailey seemed calm and relaxed for once.

"And none of us has a clue what we want to be when we grow up!" I added.

We all cracked up.

"TEAM ONE—WHAT IS SO FUNNY OVER THERE? DO YOU WANT TO SHARE A JOKE WITH THE CLASS?"

I spoke up, but not as loudly as Mr. Dooley. "Sorry, sir. We're just happy because we decided on our team name."

"Would you like to share *that* with the class?"

"Sure. It's Team Triple T."

"TEAM TRIPLE T, HUH? THAT SOUNDS LIKE A GOODIE TO ME. IT'S FRESH, YET MYSTERIOUS. GOOD USE OF ALLITERATION. TEAM ONE IS NOW TEAM TRIPLE T." Mr. Dooley went up to the whiteboard, crossed out "Team One," and wrote "Triple T."

The Tolleys turned and scowled.

"Guess they don't like our new name," Amber said.

"I've never known a Tolley twin to like anything . . . or *anybody*." Bailey sneered in the Tolleys' direction. "And they've been in my class *every* year since kindergarten." She turned to me. "Here's a tip for you, Arcade, since you're new. Whatever you do, don't ever get mixed up with Casey or Kevin Tolley."

It was great advice. But I was already mixed up to my eyebrows with Tolleys. And after reading Dad's note, I wondered if there was a way I could sharpen them. To help them . . . be better people. That would be a good thing, right?

Or maybe I just liked the challenge of becoming the first person they would ever like.

CHAPTER 11

Lunchroom Laughs

It turned out that the scratchy guy had a great sense of humor. And it's a good thing, because I accidentally called him "Scratchy" instead of Scranton in the lunch line. Couldn't help it. Ever since I saw him scratching on that first day . . . it made me laugh just thinking about it.

"Scratchy? I like that name! But, dude, I got eczema." He held out his tray for a scoop of mac & cheese. "And that stuff's no joke. You ever get that? And on top of *that*, I got a killer sunburn last week. Who knew you could get fried in New York City under all the skyscraper shade! I didn't have this problem last year when I lived in foggy Seattle."

So Scratchy was a new kid this year too. Cool.

"You wanna sit together?" Scratchy asked me. I searched the tables, but almost everywhere was full. One table had an empty chair, and a chair next to it with a coat hanging on it.

I pointed my tray that way. "Let's see what's up with the coat."

The coat belonged to a foreign exchange student from our class named Ivan. He nodded a bunch, and when I pointed to the coat, he took it off the chair and put it on the back of his. He smiled a lot during our conversation.

"So, what's the name of your team, Scratch?"

"We're calling ourselves Job Speedway. We're all about mechanics and engines and . . ."

"Speed?"

"Yeah! Haha! How'd you guess?" Scratchy took a bite of food and talked through the chewing. "I'm working on super-charging my electric scooter right now. Could be faster than taking the subway. And much more fun. We should get together sometime, and I'll take you for a ride."

Scratchy then proceeded to tell me more than I ever thought there was to know about electric scooters.

Ivan leaned forward to listen and seemed to be excited about everything Scratchy said. He kept pointing to himself and saying, "Me. Yes. Me."

Scratchy laughed. "Yes, you too, Ivan. I'll take you for a ride too."

Scratchy was a fun guy, just as I suspected. He uses the words RADICAL and RAD a lot. Like when we finished eating, Scratchy held up his hand for a high-five. "See you back in class, Arcade. Arcade . . . that's such a RADICAL name."

And Ivan, he just reached over to shake my hand and wouldn't let it go, until my palm got so sweaty it just slipped out of his grasp.

And then one of the Tolleys walked out of the lunchroom with me.

"Hey," I said, trying to fish for which twin this was. "How do I tell you guys apart, anyway? There has to be something different about you. A mole, a chipped tooth, a lazy eye, what is it?"

The Tolley twin grunted. "I don't get why people have such a hard time with us. But since you're working on my project for me, I'll give *you* a hint." He curled his finger, and I leaned in. "I'm the mean one." He started howling and ran to catch up with his brother.

"That was no help!" I yelled. And then I watched as the brothers talked to one another, pointed at me, and kept laughing. Well, at least they weren't scowling this time. Maybe I was wearing them down.

CHAPTER 12

Ivy Park Park

Turns out Ivy Park Park isn't too far from my apartment. It's in the opposite direction from the route I take to school. There's a small playground, a couple of benches, and a walking path, but not much grass. Just enough for the dogs to do their thing on it, with a plastic bag dispenser right in the middle for owners to use to clean everything up.

Doug decided he'd better go get his braces after all, so he wasn't there, and as soon as I got to the park, I received a group text from Bailey saying she couldn't make it due to "family drama." I responded with a thumbs-up emoji, and then realized that might be a mistake. I didn't mean thumbs up to the drama. Oh well. Emojis are confusing.

Amber came with her dog—a chocolate lab named Snickers. Zoe showed up right on time with Loopy, who grabbed a discarded baby pacifier off the path and brought it to Amber.

Amber knelt down to take the gift from Loopy. "Your dog is so sweet," she said, and then she picked him up. He licked her right on the lips.

"That's so disgusting," Zoe covered her mouth.

"Loopy!" I grabbed him back from Amber. "You gotta work on having better manners."

Amber waved off the comment. "It's okay. He brought me a gift before he kissed me." She giggled. "And anyway, I love animals."

Zoe reached out her hand to Amber. "Hi, I'm Zoe. Arcade's sister."

Amber smiled. "Nice to meet you. Wow, you're beautiful."

"Okay, I like you. Arcade *never* tells me that."

I leaned over and pretended to whisper in Amber's ear. "That's because she turns into a wombat after dark. You better get on home, sis, before your fangs start poking out."

Zoe reached down to pet Snickers. "Not a chance. I'm going to walk with you and learn more about your fascinating friend, Amber."

"Oh, I'd like that," Amber said. "Maybe you can help Arcade and me think of what we want to be when we grow up. There are so many things I'm interested in, I can't choose just one thing to research."

"Sounds like you and Arcade have a lot in common," Zoe said, and she gave me the googly eyes.

We started along the path with the pups. Snickers was so well trained that she stayed at Amber's right side the whole time, while Loopy ran left, right, and around my legs so that I had to stop several times to untangle myself.

Amber reached out for Loopy's leash. "Here, let me show you." She walked with him a few steps, and whenever

Loopy tried to get in front of Amber, she stopped, or she turned back around. “You have to let him know who’s boss.” She handed the leash back to me, and for a few steps, Loopy behaved.

“Hey, Amber, I was talking to my cousin Derek on the phone, and he mentioned that he might want to be a veterinarian one day. What about that? It would make a cool display at the career expo. You could bring Snickers. The kids would all love her.”

Amber nodded. “Yes, that’s on my list. And it’s in the medical field with the best patients of all—animals.” She smiled wide. “But I also have an interest in law enforcement.”

Whoa. That surprised me.

“I have a strong sense of justice.” Amber sighed. “It’s so hard to choose.”

“I know what you mean. It doesn’t make sense that we each have to choose just one.” Right about then, Loopy tied me up again. “Loop! What are you doing? You’re acting crazy today, even for you.” I put down the leash handle and used both hands to untangle my feet from the rope. And as soon as I did, Loopy took off.

“Arcade! Your dog’s gone mad.” Zoe ran after Loopy, but he was already off the path and down an embankment.

“Loopy! Come back here! Where are you going?” I threw my hands up in the air.

And then Snickers took off, with Amber running right next to her. “It’s okay, we go jogging all the time.”

“Sorry for all the drama,” I said as I caught up to Amber. “My dog is not making sense at all.”

We ran about an eighth of a mile down the Ivy Park Park path, and my heart pumped and pounded. I closed my hand around my Triple T token to keep it from bouncing against my chest, and it was blazing hot.

And then we ran right into a glitter cloud.

CHAPTER 13

K-9 Catastrophe

Amber screamed. I couldn't see a thing at first. The glitter was really thick this time.

"Don't worry, Amber," I said. But I didn't mean it, because I *was* worried. All of a sudden, we were caught up with Zoe and Loopy at the bottom of the embankment.

The doors appeared. They were wider this time, but the coin slot sat right in the middle, pulsing away, it seemed like right into my chest.

"*Not* a good idea, Arcade," Zoe put one hand on her hip and the other on her forehead. "We've got the dogs *and* Amber with us."

"What's not a good idea?" Amber held Snickers' leash and put her hand out to catch a palm full of falling glitter. She seemed mesmerized by what she was seeing.

"Uh, well, there's this token . . ." I pulled it out from under my shirt, and Amber covered her mouth when she saw the pulsing light.

She pointed to the coin slot. "And it goes in *there*?"

"See?" I said to Zoe. "Amber knows what's up."

"And Amber wasn't at the rodeo or on the TV set now, was she?"

Amber gasped. "You went to a *rodeo*? That sounds like fun."

"IT. WAS. NOT. FUN." Zoe stomped a foot with each word. She sounded just like Mr. Dooley.

Glitter swirled around the doors, and Loopy chased it around, snapping and barking at the twirling pieces. A surge of excitement shot through me, and I got real brave for a minute.

"Let's just try it again, Zoe." I pulled on the token, and it came off the chain, just like before. "Happy travels, remember? And, it was kinda fun last time."

Zoe yelled, "Noooo!"

But this was no time to listen to wombats. I stepped forward, reached for the slot, and caught my breath. The token went in, and I made the door-parting motion with my hands. They opened, and Amber, who was up for anything, apparently, and I jumped in. Zoe dragged along behind us.

The sign on the door says Pawsitive Pet Care Center. Zoe, Amber, and I stand in front of it, wearing scrubs. Mine are blue, with multicolored dog paws on them. Zoe's are orange with hummingbirds. And Ambers are red, white, and blue, with horses. I'm holding Loopy, who is all of a sudden calm, and Snickers stands at Amber's side, trying to nudge the door open with her nose.

"What is this place?" Zoe asks.

"It's the Pawsitive Pet Care Center," I answer, pointing at the sign. "See?"

"Well, duh, I can see that." Zoe looks around and jumps back when she sees me and Amber. "Whoa! You two look different!"

I glance over at Amber. She's about a foot taller than she was a few minutes ago, she's wearing some makeup, I think, and her hair is pulled back away from her face. She looks like a grown-up version of the Amber I met a few days ago.

I stare down at my arms, which are hairier than I remember. I rub my chin. It's rough with . . . stubble?

What *is* this place?

Before we have a chance to move, a woman comes out the door of the pet center to greet us.

"Oh, good, you're back! We have an emergency! One of our officers is sick." The woman reaches out to take Loopy from me, and she grabs the handle of Snickers' leash. "I'll watch the kids while you take over. Samson's in exam room two." She pushes the door open and we follow her in.

Zoe, Amber, and I look at each other in confusion.

The woman goes on, "He hasn't been keeping food down, and he's dropped a lot of weight. No bowel activity either."

Amber blurts out, "Sounds like an intestinal blockage. Have you taken an X-ray?"

The woman, who I now see has a name badge on that says Kate, opens the door of a small office and leads Loopy and Snickers in. "I'll bring you cuties some treats in a minute." Then she closes the door and stands with her back to it. "Not yet. I'll get him on a gurney and bring him to the X-ray room right away. Oh, Doctor, I'm so relieved that you're here. Frank is worried."

She's looking at Amber.

"It will be fine," Amber replies. "Samson's a hero, and we're going to take good care of him."

Kate takes off down the hallway, and Zoe and I stand there with Amber, going nuts.

"Amber, are you a DOCTOR?" I scratch my head. "Where did you come up with all that intestinal blockage stuff? And who's Samson?"

Amber grins and giggles and walks back toward the front office. She fumbles around on a desk for a file, and nods as she picks one up. "Samson's a K-9 officer. A beautiful black and brown German Shepherd. Frank is his human partner, and Samson has saved his life countless times." Amber shakes her head. "I *don't know* how I know that."

Zoe points up to a wall plaque. "But here's how you know about the intestinal blockage."

The plaque says Amber Diane Lin. Doctor of Veterinary Medicine. Cornell University.

"Okay, so you're smart," I say.

"And a vet." Zoe smiles. "I wonder what *year* this is?"

I check the little block calendar on the desk. "It says May 29, but it doesn't specify a year. It has to be at least . . . let me see . . . judging by this beard I'm growing, I've got to be about twenty-five." I shake my head as my brain searches for answers.

When did I start shaving?

A man in a New York City Police uniform comes down the hall to join us in the office.

"Hi, Frank," Amber says, and she shakes his hand.

Frank? She knows this guy? ***THIS IS CRAZY SAUCE***.

"Amber, I need that dog to live."

Amber pats the officer on the shoulder. "He will. I'm going to go make sure of it."

Kate yells from the hallway. "We're ready in X-ray, Doctor."

Amber smiles at Frank. "Let's go take a look, shall we?" Then she turns to me. "You coming, Doctor?" She points to another plaque on the wall. It says . . .

WHAT*????*

Arcade Livingston—Doctor of Veterinary Medicine.

Noooooo! I was going to be a Marine Biologist! Oh, whoops, no I wasn't. Something about cold, salty water.

"Zoe," Amber asks, "can you stay here and answer phones? I'll need Kate to help me prep the operating room if the X-rays confirm my suspicion."

Zoe's mouth drops open. "O . . . kay."

I lean over to my sister and whisper, "I don't see a certificate on the wall for you. Guess you didn't study hard enough. Heehee . . . have fun with the phones."

She shoves me toward the hallway. "Have fun with dog intestines."

Amber grabs a clipboard from her desk and gestures down the hallway. "Let's go take care of our boy." She acts like she's been doing this for years instead of just minutes.

*How can she be so **CALM**?!?!?!?*

Frank takes the lead and walks fast toward a room at the end of the hallway. Amber stops and grabs my elbow.

"I don't know what that token thing was all about, and I don't know where we are or why we're here right now. But it's pretty cool, don't you think?" Her face is glowing, and I notice that she has glitter in her eyeshadow and lip gloss.

"Amber, do you know how to OPERATE on a DOG?"

She laughs. "Of course. And so do you. You saw the certificate on the wall."

I start to shake. "I'm pretty sure I DON'T! I had to get two stitches on my finger a year ago, and I fainted."

"For real?"

"Well, I was on the floor. And they had to shove some bad-smelling stuff up my nose."

"But that's when you were just a little kid. Look at you now." She holds her palms up and smiles.

I pull my scrub shirt out from my chest.

Please, please, please be there, Triple T token.

But it's not. All I see is a bunch of new CHEST HAIR. Oh, man, this is really going DOWN!

Amber opens the door to the X-ray room.

"Here we gooooooooo!"

CHAPTER 14

Fetch the Ball

We stand in the dark room, and Amber surveys the X-rays that are hanging up in front of the light box. She points to a mass that is definitely plugging Samson's tube things—I mean, his intestines.

"Exactly as I thought," she says. "He's got a blockage. It doesn't look like a tumor though." She turns to Frank. "Did he swallow something, like maybe a toy, recently?"

Frank rubs Samson between the ears. "Well, buddy? What did you eat?" He thinks a minute. "We were at the dog park a couple of days ago, and he was chasing a little ball around with a small dog. The owner couldn't find it later." He puts his face near Samson's. "Did you really eat a *ball*?" Then he looks up at Amber. "You know about his terrible eating habits. He got in trouble for that a lot in the academy."

Amber moves in closer to inspect the X-ray again. "That could be a ball. But whatever it is, it's really plugging him up. We'll know more when we go in. And I suggest we do it now." She pushes on Samson's belly, and Samson whines a little. "Kate, did you weigh him?"

Kate reads from a computer screen in the corner. "Yes, he's down ten pounds from his last checkup."

"Oh, dear. He's dehydrated too, I am sure. Okay, go ahead and prep the ER. Arcade, we better go scrub up."

"Amber, are you SURE you know how to OPERATE on a DOG? OPERATE! ON A DOG!"

I pump soap into my hands and rub, like I do at home all the time, but this time, it's not because I'm about to eat dinner. I'm about to perform SURGERY.

Amber flips some water in my face and laughs. "You sound like Doug! Actually, I'm not *really* sure, but I have to trust what that certificate says, right? Amber Diane Lin—Doctor of Veterinary Medicine. That's me, and here I am in a veterinarian's office. I can't let a few doubts steal my identity, and neither should you."

"But we're getting ready to OPERATE on a DOG! And not just ANY dog! Samson's a POLICE OFFICER!"

Amber breathes in deep and looks at the ceiling. "Which makes this whole thing *even* better. I love K-9s so much! I've watched at least a hundred videos about them online." Then she looks at me. "Don't worry, Arcade. Just trust. Can't you see? We're caught up in some kind of magical scenario here with your special token. I'm not sure how this happened or how everything will turn out." Amber shakes her wet hands and grabs a towel to dry herself off. "We just need to go fetch a ball."

"OUT OF A DOG'S BELLY!"

Amber puts her fingers in her ears. "Now you're talking like Mr. Dooley. And the ball isn't in his belly, it's in his intestines."

And with that, Amber walks toward the ER. I follow.

Trust. Don't let doubts steal your identity.

You are Arcade Livingston. Doctor of Veterinary Medicine.

The surgery lasts about two hours. And the only thing that weirds me out is when I have to shave Samson's belly before we cut into him.

"Guess Kate didn't have time for this." Amber hands me the razor. "You might want to trim your chin while you're at it."

I truly can't remember *ever* shaving my chin. I'm only eleven. Well, at least I was an hour or so ago.

What time is it, anyway?

I look up at the clock on the wall, but there's a hazy, glittery sheen over it. I think it says it's six o'clock.

Zoe and I are late for dinner.

I try to imagine the conversation when we try explaining to our parents where we've been.

"I was in the ER shaving a dog before I cut into him to unblock his intestines."

Woo! Yeah! That's a good one, Arcade.

"Okay, here we are. Yep, it's a hard-but-spongy mass—looks like the insides of a toy ball. His stomach acid must have taken care of the outside cover." I'm totally into this surgery thing. I reach in with the instruments I am sure are called forceps and pull the ball out of Samson.

Amber applies pressure to stop the bleeding, but after several minutes, she realizes she can't. "Take a look at this, Arcade. Several inches of his intestines are destroyed. The ball must have moved up and down a lot when his body was trying to reject it. I don't think we can repair this part."

The blood is pooling. More and more of it. We have to make a decision. Fast. I say a quiet prayer for Samson to survive. And maybe for that token to appear back on the chain with the coin slot in front of me. Right now.

Andre, the animal anesthesiologist, comes over to my side. "Do you need more time? I can give him some extra juice."

I examine the wounded intestines. "Yes, I agree with Dr. Lin. We need to remove about eight inches." I look over at Samson's sleeping face. "Hope you're having a good dream, buddy, because your nap is going to be a bit longer than expected."

Dr. Lin. I can't believe I'm saying these words! I feel like I'm watching someone else perform surgery on this police dog. And though the token doesn't reappear, I'm not freaked out about it. I'm just focused on saving his life. And for some reason, for the next hour and a half, I know how to cut damaged intestines out of a dog, pull the good parts together, and stitch them up.

Zoe's never going to believe this!

CHAPTER 15
Phones and Cones

"Well, it's about time you got out here." Zoe's fists are shoved into her hips as she greets us out in the main office of the Pawsitive Pet Care Center. "Phones have been ringing off the hook. You would never believe the trouble these animals are getting themselves into! I've got a puppy who ate ant stakes, a dog with a burr in his eye—his EYE—and a cat that's all torn up from fighting with another cat. I'm glad I own a bird."

"Birds are no picnic either," I say. "They can get fatty liver disease, lipomas, bumblefoot, and let's not even talk about feather picking . . ."

Zoe closes her eyes and shakes her head. "Who *are* you and *what* are you saying to me right now?"

I point to the certificate. "Arcade Livingston, Doctor of Veterinary Medicine. And I just recited some frequent health maladies of cockatoos. And it's pretty amazing that I know something you don't for a change."

Zoe just glares and says with her French accent, "*Tu es fou.*"

Whatever that means.

"Where's Frank?" Amber asks Zoe.

Zoe puts her hand on her forehead. "I'm sorry. I was so wrapped up in animal drama that I didn't even ask about Samson. Is he going to be okay? Frank's outside with a bunch of New York City police officers. They were in here earlier, telling me stories about Samson. Had me in tears. They finally went outside since there were so many of them."

I look at Amber. "Would you like to tell them the good news, Dr. Lin?"

"Absolutely."

We walk out the doors, and twelve pairs of eyes focus on Amber. She looks confident. Professional. And I would never say this to a *living soul*, but she also looks pretty. Her mouth turns up in a grin. "Samson ate a ball. But Doctor Livingston here got it out. He also removed eight inches of intestine, which Samson can live without. We'll keep him here tonight and call you tomorrow when he's ready to go. He'll be on pain meds and muscle relaxers for a little while, and he'll have to wear a cone so he doesn't lick at his wound. But he should be back fighting crime in two to four weeks."

Frank steps forward to hug Amber, and then . . . me. "Thank you so much for saving my partner."

"You're welcome," I say, and I think it's cool that I'm as tall and as muscular as this policeman.

He steps back. "Why have I never met you before? Whenever we're here for a check-up we only see Dr. Lin."

I try not to make eye contact. "Uh . . . I recently moved here from Virginia."

"Well, then, welcome to the Big Apple! And if you ever

need my help for *anything*, please give me a call. Frank Langdon, 20th Precinct."

I nod. "I'll do that, Frank. And thanks to you all . . ." I gesture to the group. "For keeping our city safe."

Suddenly I'm bombarded with strong handshakes and the smell of manly aftershave. I'm going to have to get me some of that if my token doesn't return soon.

After a few more minutes of conversation, Amber yawns. "It's been a long day, and we've got to get things ready for the night shift." She shakes Frank's hand. "I love your dog. Some time I'd like to come check out that K-9 academy."

"The invitation is open anytime."

"Great. I'll see you tomorrow when you come to get Samson."

Tomorrow? Does she think we're just going to hang out here in token land forever?

Zoe is waiting inside for us with Loopy and Snickers. She's feeding them treats and chowing on a bowl of candy herself. "So, what do we do now? We have a bunch of pet owners to call back, and a recovering German Shepherd police officer in the back room." She turns to me. "You can make those doors appear anytime, Mr. Bumblefoot."

I reach for my chest and feel nothing but hair. "No, Zoe, I can't. I don't have the token, and I don't have any idea how to make it come back."

"Whoa, it's nine o'clock," Amber says. "Do you think we should call our parents?"

"And what would you tell your parents?" Zoe laughs. "That you're all grown up, and you're sorry you're late for dinner but you had to do emergency surgery on a German Shepherd?"

"I'll tell them I'm with Arcade working on our career expo project, and time got away from us."

"Yeah, something like fifteen years got away from us!" Goosebumps cover my whole body. "I can't believe I operated on a dog!" I feel dizzy. I take my phone out of my pocket and stare at the screen. Amber and Zoe look at their phones too.

"Glitter," Zoe says. "All I see is glitter on my screen."

"Mine has it too," Amber looks over at me.

"Mine too!"

And then a whole bunch of it falls from the sky. Loopy barks and jumps up to try and eat it.

"Don't do that Loop, you'll get sick!" As I reach down to pick him up, I feel something tickling my chest hair.

Doors with a flashing golden coin slot appear right there in the Pawsitive Pet Care Center's front office.

"Take Snickers' leash," I say to Amber.

I pass Loopy over to Zoe, and I grab the pulsing token. It comes off the chain, just like before, and I slide it in the slot. I put my hands together and gesture for the doors to open.

"Get us outta here!" I yell.

The doors open and all of us step in. Dr. Amber Lin; Zoe, the front desk phone girl; Loopy; Snickers; and me, Arcade Livingston, Doctor of Veterinary Medicine.

CHAPTER 16

On The Way Back . . .

We don't get thrown right back, like last time. This time we go for a ride.

We're in a large room, and the lady—the old one from the library—is there in front of me. But it's like she's in a movie, or it's a hologram of her. And she keeps saying, "Happy travels, Arcade" so loudly that my ears hurt worse than when Mr. Dooley talks.

"Who are you?" I call to her, and then I hear a deep, devilish laugh coming from behind me.

"It's not yours!" the lady yells. "Leave him alone!"

I slump down and squeeze my eyes shut, but I can feel a kind of shadow covering me.

"Give me the token! You stole it!"

"The token belongs to the boy," the lady says. "Don't listen to him, Arcade. He'll only have the power if you give it to him!"

"What power?"

And then the room goes black and begins to drop like an elevator.

CHAPTER 17

No Place Like Ivy Park Park

I hit the ground hard. Good thing I landed on one of the few grassy patches in New York City.

"Zoe? Amber?" I sat up and rubbed my head. And when I did, I noticed that my arms were back to their original size and non-hairiness.

Loopy jumped on my lap, climbed up my chest, and began licking my nose. I hugged him with all my might.

"Arcade, are you all right? We've been looking all over for you! I thought you didn't make it back." Now Zoe was down on the ground hugging Loopy and me, and even kissing me on the forehead. Gross. "I'm sorry I called you a bumblefoot. I don't even know what that is."

Amber stood there, watching the sisterly slobber-fest. Snickers too. "Hello, Doctor Livingston."

I stood up and brushed myself off. I looked around. "Are we back at Ivy Park Park?"

Zoe made a sob-laughing sound. "Yeah, it looks like it." She grabbed her forehead. "And it's still light out."

Amber checked her phone. "It's only four-fifteen. And

it appears we're right back where we started when we ran into that glitter cloud."

Goosebumps rose on my arms. "Did you see the lady?"

Zoe looked around in confusion and shrugged. "What lady?"

"The one who gave me the token. She was yelling at the shadow and then the room fell . . ."

Zoe reached over and placed her hand on my forehead. "You're burning up. Are you feeling okay? I didn't see any lady. Did you, Amber?"

Amber shook her head. "When did you see her, Arcade?"

"It was right after we went through the doors. She was in the room, and her voice was really loud."

"Zoe and I stepped right through the doors and onto this grass. *You* didn't show up for a few minutes after that. You didn't perform any dog surgeries without me, did you?"

"No, I would never . . ." Goosebumps covered me again, and I felt exhausted. Or worried? No, it was something else.

"Arcade?" Zoe waved her hands in front of my eyes. "Hello? Are you there?"

My heart raced, and my hands got all clammy. I turned my head as far as I could—right, then left—searching for something, but I didn't know what. Loopy jumped and barked, so I picked him up. He whined and stretched to lick my neck.

"I-I'm okay. But, w-we n-need to get out of here."

Amber took hold of Snickers' leash and we all began to walk-jog out of Ivy Park Park.

"Amber," Zoe said, "Arcade and I really don't know what's going on with the token, so if you could not say anything to . . ."

"Your secret is safe with me," Amber covered her heart with her right hand. "Plus, if I tried to tell anyone what just happened, who would believe me?"

No one would. Except maybe Frank. And Samson the K-9. If they actually existed.

CHAPTER 18

Some Explaining to Do

The walk home was a blur. Amber split off from us at some point, but I wasn't paying attention to where or when. Her calm, "See you tomorrow," rang in my ears for the rest of the way home—along with other thoughts that pounded away in my brain:

"Happy travels."

"Enjoy the ride."

"He'll only have the power if you give it to him."

"What power?" I blurted out loud.

Zoe grabbed my elbow and pulled me to a stop, just before we rounded the last corner to our brownstone.

"Arcade, what's *going on* with you? You're scared, I can tell."

That's it! That's the feeling.

Fear.

I looked her in the eyes. "There's someone after me. Or after the token, I think. The old lady warned me in the room. She said not to give him the power."

Zoe felt my forehead again. "I don't know, Arcade. You're still hot. Are you sure you didn't dream that part?"

I pushed her hand down. "Did you dream answering phones at the Pawsitive Pet Care Center?"

Zoe bit her lip. "No, I didn't." She looked behind me and then turned. "Let's get to the house."

As we climbed the steps to our front door, Zoe briefed me on what to say to our parents that evening. "Say *nothing,* Arcade. And I *mean* it! I'll tell them you're sick, and then I'll bring food up to your room. When we finally figure this all out, we can tell them what's going on."

Seemed like a good plan to me. But things don't always go according to plan.

Inside, we were greeted by two notes. One from Dad:

> *Hey guys, had to go to work early tonight. Stage malfunction. Love, Dad.*

And one from Mom:

> *Got called to a meeting. So sorry! Take and Bake pizza in the fridge. Cook for 20 minutes. 400 degrees. Love you so much! Mom.*

Zoe sighed and dumped her backpack on the dining room chair. "Good. Now we can relax and figure out what's going on with that Triple T token."

"Triple T! Triple T!"

I slumped down on the couch. "*Now* you did it! Milo can't keep a secret. Time for a hamster."

Zoe walked over to Milo's cage, opened the door, and took him out. He leapt from her finger to her shoulder.

"Milo's a smart birdy," she said.

"Smart birdy! Smart birdy!"

Zoe smoothed some of Milo's ruffled feathers. "Don't worry, Arcade, he'll forget. I'll teach him some new stuff, and we won't say that other thing again." She petted him on the head. "You want some pizza, Milo?"

Milo jerked his head back and forth and pecked at his chest feathers.

I pointed at him. "Hey, look! Feather picking! I think he needs a vet. We could drop him off at the Pawsitive Pet Care Center and leave him there till this thing blows over. And that could take years."

Zoe's eyes grew wide. "Hey, Arcade! Do you think the Pawsitive Pet Care Center *actually* exists?" She grabbed Milo off her shoulder and had him back in the cage in seconds. Then she ran over to her backpack, took out her phone, and started poking at the screen.

"Huh? What are you talking about? I was just kidding." I scratched my head and tried to get up from the couch.

And then, a knock at the door. Zoe snapped her fingers at me and pointed in that direction, while still checking her phone.

"Okay, I'll get it!" I wish I hadn't. Because there on the steps stood a Tolley twin. He was big and wrinkled as usual.

"Uh, hey, yeah." He looked around while wringing his hands. "Can I come in?"

In? Like, into my house?

I didn't have a chance to decline. Mr. Tolley shoved himself in. Practically knocked me over with my own door.

"Oops! Sorry about that." He reached over to smooth my shirt. "I had to duck my brother."

"And *you* are?" Zoe stood and stared at the Tolley twin, with a hand on her hip.

Tolley looked at me and pointed a finger toward Zoe. "What is *she* doing here?"

Zoe cleared her throat and gave the twin a nasty glare. "I *live* here. What are *you* doing here? Welcoming us to the neighborhood?"

"Uh, no. Nothing like that."

Zoe rolled her eyes.

"Me and Arcade have a meeting."

I raised my eyebrows. "We do?"

The twin nodded. "Yeah, we do. But we gotta make it quick. Can we go somewhere . . . private?"

Zoe put her phone up to her ear.

"You two could go up to Arcade's room." She pointed up the stairs.

Next thing I knew, I had a Tolley *in my room*. I'd get Zoe back for that later.

"You got the outline and the plans yet? I picked up some pallets from the dumpster and I want to start building."

Casey.

"Not yet. I had a little delay after school and I haven't been feeling well."

"Hey—what is *this*?" Casey walked over to my desk and picked the top book off the large stack. "Man, you really *are* a bookworm!" The book he picked up was about card tricks and illusions.

"Is this a job I could have? Illusionist?"

Sure. And could you make yourself disappear right now?

I watched as he opened up to the first page.

Or . . . maybe I could be the one who creates an illusion instead.

I walked over to him and took the book out of his hands. "Nah, this wasn't what I was thinking for you. Actually . . ." I spied the book on specialized treehouses halfway down the stack. Derek and I once talked about living in one together when I move back to Virginia someday.

I pulled the book out and showed him some of the color photos. "Casey, since you like to build, why not build something cool and unique . . . like you are?" No hurt in building the guy up. After all, there was no one *quite* like him. Even though he had a twin, there had to be *some* differences. I searched his neck for moles.

"You think I'm cool and unique?" Casey took the book back from me and began flipping through the pages. "Dude, I could build ziplines too?"

I pointed out a picture of a deluxe treehouse with a zipline coming out of it. "Well, yeah, ziplines work best with trees, so that's included in this kind of work. But it takes a lot of special training, and while I'm sure you are quite talented, I wonder if you would have the focus and drive to do this job well. So I'm researching other jobs for you."

I reached to take the book, but Casey yanked it back. "Hey, I got the drive." He pointed to his temple. "And the smarts!"

I shook my head. "I don't know. I think you should stay with something simpler. It would make an awesome display, though. Maybe you could . . ." I put my finger to my lips.

"Maybe I could what?"

"Nah, you wouldn't want to do it."

"How do you know? Tell me!"

The big guy is falling for this.

"Well, Casey, I was thinking, but since I'm not an expert, I wouldn't even know how to outline this or write it up or even what materials, tools, or training you would need . . ."

Casey walked right up to my face. "Tell me, Arcade."

"Okay, okay. What if you built a small zipline for the career expo? It could be low to the ground, but you could hook the kids up and let them ride it. But nah—it would be too hard. Never mind."

Casey cracked a smile. First time I had seen that. And he did have a small chip on his right upper tooth! Something to tell him apart. But not totally helpful, because the Tolley twins don't make a habit of smiling.

"That would be sweeeeet! My team would win with that, for sure." Casey turned to another page in the book. "These pictures are amazing! I can't wait to get started on this."

I held my hands out. "Oh, wait a minute. *I'm* doing this, remember?" I grabbed the book, and then I found myself in a tug-of-book with Casey Tolley.

And then we dropped it. It landed on my foot.

Casey scowled. "Now look what you did! I hope you didn't wreck the book!" Glad to see that he had some respect for library books, if not for smashed feet.

I picked the book up off my foot and handed it to Casey. "Okay, since you have so much interest in this, I'll make you a deal."

"But *you* don't make the deals, I do." Casey moved closer to me, almost bumping my chest with his.

I backed up a couple of steps and sucked in some air. "I get that. Just hear me out a second. What if *you* do this *first part* of the project?"

Casey moved back. "Yeah, why not? I could do a better job than you anyway."

I breathed out. "But when you finish, you *have* to check in with me, okay? I only turn in quality work."

"Oh, it'll be quality." Casey pulled opened the book again and scanned a page. "But you'll have to make sure everything's spelled right so I get an A on this thing."

"Okay, I'll do whatever you say." I showed Casey the time on my phone. "Hey, is Kevin out looking for you? You better get back home!" I opened my closet and pulled out an old, Loopy-chewed backpack that somehow made it through the move. "Put the book in here. You don't want anyone to know you're reading about this interesting stuff. They might steal your idea."

Casey took the backpack. "Yeah. And don't *you* tell anybody."

I put both hands up. "Your secret's safe with me." I smiled. Amber had said those words just a little while ago.

Casey put his face near mine and narrowed his eyes before taking off down the inside stairs and landing in the living room, where Zoe was engaged in some sort of conversation on her phone.

"You never saw me," Casey said to Zoe, and then he disappeared.

Zoe hung up from her call. "What was *that* all about?"

"Just making friends with the neighbors."

Zoe smirked. "Yeah, right. I think he just stole your ratty backpack. But, who cares about that right now because . . . the Pawsitive Pet Care Center *exists*! Check this out! It's over on West 83rd Street!"

I grabbed the phone from her to look at her screen. Sure enough, she had a website up for Pawsitive Pet Care Center. And there was a picture . . . with the same door and sign on the front!

"And, guess what? I made an appointment to take Milo in for his feather picking."

My mouth dropped open. "Zoe, we can't go there!"

"Why not?"

"They'll recognize us! And then arrest me for doing dog surgery when I'm only eleven."

"But you *weren't* eleven when you did the surgery. Plus, you had a license. *And* it was successful, right? They won't recognize you."

I felt my chin. Definitely no stubble. And then I thought about ball-eating Samson and Officer Frank. "Hey, Zoe! Do you think Frank Langdon is real? And working at the 20th precinct? Do you think he would try to find me if Samson gets sick again?"

Zoe threw her hands in the air. "Who knows how this token thing works? But even if he *were* real, I doubt he could find you."

Goosebumps rose all over my body. Again. Oh, he could find me. He's a policeman. How many Arcade Livingstons *are* there in the world? And how many *in* New York City?

And if he found me, I'd have a whole lot of explaining to do!

CHAPTER 19

Triple T Tuesday

I spent most of Monday night reading. Scanned through at least twenty-five books. Each contained great ideas for the career expo, but I couldn't focus on one book long enough to decide on a career for me or the members of my team. Every time I got excited about something, I remembered that shadow, and the fear grew until I had to get up and move, grab another book, or pace around my room.

"I HAVE BEEN HEARING EXCITING CAREER IDEAS FROM SOME OF YOU."

Good thing Mr. Dooley's Tuesday voice was thundering. He was keeping me awake.

"BUT THE REST OF YOU—REMEMBER THAT YOUR OUTLINE IS DUE NEXT FRIDAY. THE LONGER YOU TAKE TO DECIDE, THE LESS TIME YOU HAVE TO MAKE YOUR PROJECT GREAT. I'M GIVING YOU AN HOUR RIGHT NOW TO WORK IN YOUR TEAMS, SO GET ON IT!"

"Arcade, are you all right?" Amber reached over and

tapped my desk with her pencil. "You've been zoned out most of the morning."

I shook my head, let my cheeks go slack, and made a blubbering noise. "I think dog surgery took a lot out of me."

Amber giggled. "Hey, I decided what to do for my career project."

"No joke? Let me guess. Doctor of Veterinary Medicine?"

She shook her head. "Nope."

"Really? Then what?"

Doug and Bailey dragged their chairs over and interrupted our conversation.

"Arcade, will you tell Doug that he can't be an inventor of Gummy Braces for our project? That would be so lame."

Doug smiled big to show off his new mouth design. A full set of braces with bright blue and green rubber bands. "I say it's *not* lame." Doug pointed to his mouth. "Can you imagine looking this great in your braces, *and* being able to eat whatever you want?"

"Anything's possible, Bailey," I said. "And what would you put in your display, Doug?"

Doug pulled a bag of gummy worms out of his backpack. "Candy."

"That's *it*?" Bailey palmed her forehead.

"Would I need anything else? We're talking kids here." Doug opened the bag, put his nose in, and sniffed.

Amber took her project guideline booklet out of her notebook. "If you want a good grade, you may want to consider other possibilities."

"Hey, Amber has a good idea for her project." I scooted my chair up closer to my desk and sat up straight to listen.

Bailey picked at her pencil eraser. "Oh, *please* tell us, Amber. Team Triple T could really use a boost right now."

Amber opened her booklet up to the page where we were supposed to list our career choice. "I would like to propose that my career be Trainer for K-9 Officers in New York City."

Of course! That would be perfect for Amber. She had a special instinct with dogs. Loopy actually listened to her better than to me!

"I've been watching a lot of videos online, and I checked into visiting a place in the city that serves as a local K-9 academy. I have an appointment to go next week. What do you all think?"

"What do we all think?" Doug still had his nose in the gummy worm bag.

"Yes," Amber said. "I want to know what you all think."

I laughed. "I think it's a great idea."

Bailey had been scribbling on a notepad. She stopped, chewed her pencil a little, and looked up at the ceiling. "I like it. It's original and exciting. And everyone loves dogs. I think it's a winner." She looked around at the rest of us. "Any input for Amber on the K-9 idea?"

"I'm down for goin' to the K-9 academy," Doug said.

"Me too." Bailey wrote "Visit to K-9 academy" in her planner.

I wanted to mention that I had operated on a K-9 just

a couple of days ago. But I didn't. For obvious reasons. I grabbed for the token under my shirt.

Why can't I think of any careers for myself?

At that moment, a tightly-wrapped paper wad flew over and nailed me in the forehead. I picked it up off the floor, opened it up, and read what was written on it under my desk.

Hey—what's my project? It better be good.

I looked up and spied a Tolley glaring at me from his team gathering. He put his hands up, like he'd just delivered the game-winning strike. I gave him a forced grin and wave.

"Ha! Nice pitch, Kev!" the other Tolley yelled from his team gathering.

And it gave me an idea for Kevin.

"I got it!" Doug jumped to his feet. "I could be a candy maker! Ever see those guys who make the peanut brittle in the big vats? That's so cool! Or how about kettle corn?"

It was getting close to lunch, and Doug's suggestions made my stomach growl.

"Just more foods you can't eat with braces," Bailey said.

"Ah, RATS!" Doug slumped in his chair.

The bell rang for lunch. Mr. Dooley jumped up from his desk.

"OKAY, CLASS. TIME TO GOOOOOOOOOOOOO!"

"Well?"

Kevin Tolley was waiting for me in the lunch line. I

figured it was him because he had a couple paper wads sitting on a tray of food he had brought for me. He sort of shoved it in my gut.

"Hey, Kevin."

"My team wants to know what my career project is. So, what is it?"

"Uh . . . you want to sit together and talk about it?" I swung my head around to scan the lunchroom. Seats were filling up fast. Scratchy's table was full, and I couldn't find Doug anywhere.

That kid Ivan had an empty seat on one side of him. And an empty seat with a coat on it on the other side.

Hmmm.

I cocked my head in the direction of Ivan, and Kevin followed.

"Hey, Ivan!" I sat my tray down on the table. "You know it's not really coat weather, right? Must be eighty degrees out there."

Ivan grinned real big. Then he took his coat off the chair and put his hand out to show me I could sit there. Kevin grunted and slid his tray onto the table space on Ivan's right. Poor Ivan was going to be in the middle while we "secretly" worked on Kevin's project. Good thing he didn't speak English well.

"So about your project . . ." I leaned over to see Kevin, and I wiped my sweaty palms on my jeans.

Kevin tore a big piece of hamburger off with his teeth and chewed. "Yeah, what about it?"

"You really nailed me with that paper bomb earlier. You ever play baseball?"

Kevin swallowed. "Yeah, I played it pretty good too. I was a pitcher and no kid could hit me."

Exactly what I had hoped. "Do you still play?"

"Nah."

Ivan's head ponged back and forth, like he was watching a tennis tournament.

Kevin took a swig of milk and swallowed. "My parents took me out. Said I had to get my grades up. And they needed the money for Michael's fancy high school and voice lessons." He pointed his index finger in the air and twirled it. "Whoop-de-doo."

Ouch. I didn't know how much those high schools cost, but I knew my parents spent a lot of time budgeting so they could afford to send Zoe.

"So, you're pretty athletic then?"

Kevin pushed up his left sleeve, bent his arm, and flexed a bicep.

I opened my eyes wide and tried to act impressed. "Whoa! You work out?"

"Sure do! Made my own home gym. It's not real equipment, just stuff I found around the neighborhood. I lift, and I box, and I throw things into a tarp. I also hit rocks real far with sticks. You should come check it out sometime."

Ivan nodded his head. "Me too. Yah, me."

Kevin jostled Ivan with his shoulder. "Yeah, Ivan, you can come too."

It was exactly what I hoped would happen—that Kevin would reveal a talent. I know God gives talents to everyone, but it's hard to see it right away in bullies sometimes. "Can I come after school? Are you doing anything today?"

Kevin laughed. "Nah, I'm never doing anything. Michael does all the stuff in our family."

"Okay, then. I'll come over at four-thirty." I took a pen out of my backpack and wrote my address on a napkin. Then I handed it to Ivan. "Meet me here at four-twenty, and we can go over to Kevin's together. Okay?"

Ivan nodded a bunch. "Yah. Me too. Me."

This kid could keep me from getting beat up if my plan to trick Kevin into doing his own project backfired.

Chapter 20
Tricks and Sticks

We didn't work on our projects anymore that day. But every time I had a free minute between subjects, I found my mind searching for a career expo idea. For me.

I grabbed the token and tugged.

I just want to help people. And as weird as this is, it's been more fun for me to figure out ideas for everyone else. Why am I drawing a blank? It just doesn't make sense.

The token heated up, and I dropped it.

No, not here! Mr. Dooley is about to start our math lesson, and Zoe would be mad if I went through the doors without her.

I picked up my math book and fanned myself with it. I checked under my shirt. No pulsing light. I looked ahead of me and up. No falling glitter. Although I couldn't help but think how funny it would be to see the Tolleys showered in glitter right now.

"Are you okay?" Amber leaned over to check on me. "You're zoning again. Is your fever back?"

"No. I'm just thinking about my career project. I have no idea what to do yet."

"Don't worry. You still have time to figure it out. An idea will come. Just trust. Mine came to me in the weirdest way possible."

"You got that right."

"MR. LIVINGSTON? DO YOU HAVE A MATH QUESTION OR ARE YOU HAVING A TEA PARTY WITH MISS LIN?" The whole class laughed. Mr. Dooley was in that crossed-arm, glasses-off stance that means you're busted.

When do I not have a question? About anything?

I searched my brain database and my favorite one popped right out.

"Yes, sir, I do have a math question. I've always wanted to ask a teacher this. How many sides are on a stop sign?"

The class laughed again. One of the Tolleys formed his hand into a letter L and popped it on his forehead.

Mr. Dooley hopped up and sat on top of his desk. He put his glasses back on and pushed them up on his nose.

"THAT'S A BRILLIANT QUESTION, ARCADE. ONE I THINK WE SHOULD EXPLORE WHEN WE ARE *NOT* TALKING ABOUT ALGEBRAIC EQUATIONS."

"Duh," the other Tolley belted out. "Everyone knows it's eight."

"Oh!" Scratchy held his hand up high and scratched his leg with his other hand.

"MR. SCRANTON? IS SOMETHING ON FIRE?" Mr. Dooley pushed himself off the desk and walked over to the whiteboard where he added some letters to an equation he'd been working on.

"No, sir. I just wanted to answer Arcade's question. It's sooo easy. Ten. Ten sides on a stop sign. I'm sure of it."

I smiled.

Scratchy just might become one of my New York best buddies. Something about the way that guy thinks . . .

Zoe gave me a hard time when she caught up with me at the subway entrance on my way home from school.

"Hey, you changed your shirt! Must be Tuesday. I knew you could do it."

"Unfortunately, *you* haven't changed your lipstick color."

"I'm not wearing lipstick."

"Oh, bummer. Guess you're stuck with it then."

Zoe swung her foot out to trip me. Luckily, I didn't hit the ground.

We both laughed and continued walking down the street.

"Do you think Mom and Dad will be home when we get there today?"

Zoe kicked a rock off the sidewalk. "I don't know, Arcade. It's been a crazy adjustment for all of us. I'm afraid we better get used to heating up pizzas. Or . . ."

"Or, what?"

"I *could* start making us some French recipes that I found in the library book I got last week."

"Hmm." My stomach growled a bit. "That wouldn't be too bad. Can you make French fries?"

"Arcade, French fries are not French."

I stopped. "What?

"French fries didn't originate in France."

"Then why call them French fries?"

Zoe sighed and rolled her eyes. "Must you always ask so many silly questions?"

"That is *not* a silly question! If they didn't come from France, then the name French fries is silly!"

"*Your* name is silly. It fits you, though. Just like French fries fits. So get over it."

She had me with that one. I never could understand why

my parents named me Arcade. It sounds cool. Arcaaaaade. And no one ever has the same name as me. Mom said she'd tell me one day, when I'm older and can appreciate the story. Then she gives my dad the dreamy eyes, and I realize I can wait.

"Zoe's a weird name too. It's like Zoo, but with an e. Sometimes I'm tempted to call you Zoo. You have a lot of similarities to a zoo."

"Zoe means *life*, Arcade. I don't know how I could have a better name than that."

"Whatever."

She tripped me again and ran. And I ran after her, laughing.

We might be in a strange new city, with our parents working awful schedules, but at least the teasing from my sister made me feel normal.

We both got tired and slowed down as we rounded the last corner to our brownstone. And as often happens when we've been teasing, Zoe held out a fist, and said, "We cool?"

I hit her fist with an open hand. "Sure, turkey!"

Just then, I spotted the Tolley brothers sitting out on their steps.

"Hey, Arcaaaaade. Sister have to walk you home so you don't get lost?"

One of the twins was lifting a plastic milk jug that looked like it was filled with sand. Kevin.

Oh no! The meeting! I totally forgot.

How did I get myself into this mess? I was just minding my own business at the library. None of it made *any* sense.

"Arcade, look!" Zoe turned to face me and pointed to a dark cloud that formed above my head. I looked up and, before I knew it, glitter all over. I coughed and sputtered. I should really learn to keep my mouth closed.

"Oh no, the token! It's flashing again! What did you *do*, Arcade?"

Zoe jumped closer to me, under the glitter storm.

"If those doors show up again, *don't* go through them."

I coughed. "What?"

"Ignore them. Keep walking right back to the house."

I took my backpack off and put it over my head like an umbrella. "But what if I'm *supposed* to go through? What if I ignore it, and then my life takes some deadly turn? If I skip on the *Happy travels*, will I end up traveling anyway, but somewhere not so happy?"

"Ugh! Why are you such a question machine?"

A larger glitter cloud formed over Zoe now and dumped its contents on her head. The doors appeared again, but this time we could see through them. I was on one side, and Zoe was on the other. That coin slot was right there in the middle, pulsing away. Zoe put her hand up and realized we were separated. Her face paled and she put both hands on the doors.

"Do you still want me to ignore it?" I didn't know if she could hear me or not. "What if we get separated forever?" The token blazed heat, and the coin slot continued to pulse light toward the coin around my neck.

Tears streamed down Zoe's cheeks. She said something, but I couldn't hear her. She pounded the doors with her hands.

I couldn't ignore this! I had to get to my sister. The only way to do that was to put the token in the slot. I reached down and grabbed it. Like the last three times, it came off the chain. I reached for the slot, and the token popped in. Like it was home.

This isn't so bad. We're at Yankee Stadium. I know because we're standing in front of a massive square building that says YANKEE STADIUM.

"Why is everything black and white?" Zoe is standing next to me, and she's waving her hand in front of her eyes while looking at the sign.

"*Now* who's asking silly questions? It's just an overcast day in New York." I reach out my hand. She grabs it, and we walk in the entrance.

But as we walk down the aisles of seats, through the crowds of people, and up to the field level, it appears everything *is* black and white. Because the grass is . . . gray. And the sky is a . . . lighter gray. And all the fans sitting in the seats, the peanut guy, and the hot dogs the people are shoving in their mouths, are all either black, white, or various shades of gray.

Zoe blinks her eyes open and closed. "This is freaking me out!"

A guy wearing a gray suit approaches me. "Arcade Livingston?"

My mouth drops open. "Yeeeeeeaaaah?"

"This way. He's been looking forward to meeting you."

"He has?"

Who has?

"Yes. Who doesn't want to meet Arcade Livingston?"

I smile and turn to Zoe. "Yeah, who doesn't want to meet me?" Then I turn back to the guy in the suit. "This is my sister. Her name is Zoo. Can she come too?"

The man grins. "Yes, I'm sure he'd like to meet Zoo too. Follow me."

We follow him toward the gray field and through a gate with a sign that says "Authorized Personnel Only." We head down the steps, onto the field, where the New York Yankees—dressed in black-and-white pinstriped uniforms—are playing a game! And then we turn into the dugout, where a bunch of Yankees are spitting gray stuff on the ground and yelling things to their teammates out on the field.

"You can sit right here," our tour guide says. "He'll be in as soon as he strikes this last batter out." The man points to a couple of empty spots on a long bench, and I sit down. Zoe inspects the bench first, and then joins me.

"Hey! Are you *Arcade*? Thanks for coming to visit, man!" One of the coaches comes over and gives me a high-five. "We heard you moved to New York! Lucky us!"

A bunch of other players come over then, and high-five me too.

In the background, I hear an announcer. Sounds like Mr. Dooley.

"THREE BALLS, TWO STRIKES. AND HERE WE GOOOOOOO! THE MONEY PITCH . . ."

The ballplayers part in front of me, and I stand to see what's going on. A big guy, wearing pinstripes with the number three on his sleeve, winds up on the mound. He heaves the baseball toward the batter. He swings and misses. The baseball disappears in the catcher's glove.

"STRIKE THREE! LADIES AND GENTS, HE'S STRUCK OUT THE SIDE! AGAIN!"

The crowd roars, and the Yankees on the field run toward the dugout. The big guy comes in last and sees me.

"Arcade! Where you been?"

Huh?

"Virginia?"

He laughs. "It's about time you moved to the Big Apple." He throws his glove in a slot in the wall of the dugout. "Come over here, I want to show you something."

Zoe gives me a puzzled glance, and I smirk. "He wants to show us something."

"I heard you, Doug."

The big guy leads us over to a square table in the corner of the dugout. It's a weird thing to be there, but this whole scene is weird.

"Have a seat." He gestures to two flimsy metal chairs for me and Zoe, and I cringe as he sits down, wondering if the seat will hold him.

A deck of cards appears on the table.

"Was that the trick?' I ask with wide eyes.

"No, I haven't even started."

"But the cards just . . ."

Zoe kicks me under the table and I stop talking. Number three shuffles the cards a few times, then fans them out to show me the whole deck is there.

Like I'm going to question this big, pinstriped baseball player.

"Okay," he says. "I'm going to make three stacks of three cards." He counts them out. Since I've been reading a book about illusions and card tricks, of course I'm looking at his sleeves. But they're short, and he just came off the field, so how could he have anything up them?

The big guy presses his elbows into the table. "Okay, Arcade, pick which pile you want."

I pick the middle. I always pick middle piles.

He picks up the middle pile and turns it over. The bottom card is the jack of hearts. The card is all in black, white, and gray, but a heart is a heart.

Star pitcher takes my pile and puts it on top of the other two piles of three. He sets the rest of the deck aside. "Do you trust me to find your card?"

My answer *should* be yes, because illusionists always find your card, but I just got here through some glitter and elevator doors that open with a mysterious token. I'm not sure *what* will happen. So I say, "Mmmmmyeeaahno?"

Zoe laughs. "What my brother is trying to say is . . . Mmmmmyeeaahno." She hits her hand on the table, and it causes the big guy to jump.

"Oh, sorry! I didn't mean to startle you."

He moves a bit and his chair groans under his weight. "That's okay. A shot of adrenaline may help me when I get up to bat. I've been slumpin' today."

Then he looks at me again. "Now we're going to find that jack of hearts."

He begins to spell the word jack, and with each letter he says out loud, he puts a card face down on the table. "J-A-C-K."

Then he says "Space," and he puts the rest of the deck on top of the ones on the table.

He continues. "O-F. Space."

Again, he puts the deck on top.

He does the same thing with H-E-A-R-T-S.

"Space."

He stops for a minute and stares into my eyes. "Spelling is a very important skill. Don't forget that."

"I won't," I respond, recording his advice in my brain.

"Now," he continues, "do you trust me to find your card?"

"Yes."

He starts putting cards facedown as he spells the word trust. "T-R-U-S-"

And he turns the next card over as he says, "T."

Something hot sears my chest. I reach down and discover the token is already back. But no doors.

The card the baseball man turns over is the jack of hearts.

Zoe gasps.

"That's dope!" I check his sleeves again. I feel like I've done this one before, but I can't remember how. "So what's the trick?"

The announcer says, "NUMBER THREE ON DECK!"

The crowd roars.

The big man rises and smiles, and little lines form in the corners of both eyes. He picks up his bat and rests it on his shoulder. "That's the magic of it. There *is* no trick. You just have to be confident and trust the process."

The announcer continues. "TWO AWAY, AND HERE COMES THE BAMBINO, WHO'S DOMINATING ON THE MOUND, BUT HAVING A ROUGH TIME AT THE PLATE WITH TWO STRIKEOUTS TODAY."

"What do they expect?" The big guy takes his bat off his shoulder and points it at me. "Remember, kid. You can't be so scared of striking out that you don't swing."

And with that, he charges out on the field.

"Is that who I think it is?" Zoe asks.

"I think so. And he's gonna hit it out, you watch."

And then a bunch of glitter falls from the dugout ceiling.

"No, wait! Not yet!" I yell, but the doors appear anyway. The token pulses. So does the coin slot.

The players in the dugout are unfazed, but Zoe grabs me by the arm.

"We gotta go, Arcade."

I keep my eyes trained on the batter and push her away. "Just a minute! I want to witness history."

"If we don't go now, *we* may be history!"

The pitcher winds up and hurls a fast ball. Number three swings so hard he practically screws himself into the ground. The players in the dugout moan. The glitter increases. I have to wipe it away from my face to see.

"Arcade, come on!" Zoe's voice fades as if she's in a far-away tunnel.

The pitcher moves the ball around in his palm and repositions it in his glove. He smirks at the batter, who glares back and spits on the ground.

"EDWARDS WINDS UP . . . THE PITCH . . ."

It's a slider. Number three swings again, missing it by a foot!

"C'mon, Babe!" the manager yells. "That wasn't your pitch!"

The big guy makes a time-out sign, and he moves out of the box so he can swing a few times. Then he's back in.

"Arcaaaade, your shirt is smoking!"

Huh? I look around and don't see Zoe, but sure enough, there's a little bit of steam coming from my shirt. But I'm so into what's happening on the gray field that I can't deal with it right now.

"O AND TWO, EDWARDS FROM THE STRETCH."

The batter turns to me and winks. He says, "Don't be afraid," and I can hear him, clear as if he's standing right next to me.

"THE PITCH . . ."

The pitcher hurls another fast ball, but it looks like slow

motion to me. The batter's eyes focus on the seams, and as it nears the plate, he shifts his weight . . . and swings.

CRACK!

"Arrrrrrcaaaaaaade!"

I glance back, and Zoe is gone. I turn back toward the field, just in time to watch the little white ball sail high over the right field fence. Way over.

The crowd goes wild, and next thing I know I'm choking on glitter. The doors are still there, but I can barely see the outline. And the light from the coin slot has faded, looking like a flashlight when the battery is almost dead. I grab for the token, and this time I have to tug it for a second to get it to come off the chain. I throw it in the coin slot, and it blinks a couple of times, but then the light goes out. I put my hands together and make the open-door gesture, and . . .

Nothing.

"OPEN! You have to OPEN!" I make the motion again, and I bang on the coin slot. I look around at the players, who have run out on the field to congratulate number three on his home run. I'm in here all by myself.

Or am I?

"HAHAHAHAHAHAHAHA!" I hear that devilish laugh again. "I told you, he can't handle it."

"Yes, he can," a weaker voice says. I glance over to the card table, and there's the old lady. She's dealing out three stacks of cards. She holds up the ace of hearts and starts spelling.

"A-R-C-A-D-E. Space."

I hit the coin slot again. Make the motion. My head lets loose a gallon of sweat. "Help me!" I yell, and I fix my eyes on her card deck.

"T-R-U-S . . ." She flips the fifth card over. It's an ace, but instead of hearts in the corners, the whole card is covered in golden tokens.

I turn back around. The coin slot is glowing bright now. "Take me home. I *can* handle it!" I make the motion again.

The doors open. And I leap through.

Zoe wasn't there with me when I arrived back at the end of our block.

"Hey, Arcade! We got an appointment, remember?" Kevin still stood on the steps to his brownstone, doing biceps curls with his milk jug full of dirt. His arm looked pumped.

I pulled on my backpack straps and ran toward my house. "I'll be there in a minute! I have to check something! Just keep getting, uh, pumped!" I huffed and puffed up the stairs, and I put the key in the front door.

Please, God, let Zoe be in here!

I didn't get a chance to push it open, because someone swung it open from the inside. I sailed in and almost fell on the ground.

Zoe was chowing on ice cream out of the carton at the dining room table. She flew over and hugged me so tight I couldn't breathe. "Arcade! Thank God, you're all right!" Then she pushed me away a foot or two. "You *are* all right, aren't you?" She looked me up and down.

"I'm okay, I think. But what about you?" I swung an arm toward the door and then back toward Zoe. "When did you get . . . how did you get . . . how long . . ."

Zoe interrupted, shoving me toward the wall. "I ended up right back where we started, with those dumb see-through doors! And you weren't there, so I thought I lost you forever, and I ran back here, ready to call the cops." She pushed me again. "But then I wondered, 'What would I tell the cops if I called them?' and I freaked out! I almost called Mom, but then this kid knocked on the door and said he was looking for you, so I let him in."

"Kid? What kid?" I pushed myself off the wall and turned toward the door.

"Arcade? Me? Kevin?" Ivan was holding the doorknob.

Zoe went right back to the table and shoved a spoonful of ice cream in her mouth. Then she gave me the stink-eye and shook her head. "You should have put the token in the slot as soon as you saw the doors. That was *super dangerous*!"

I didn't want to admit she was right. But when the token didn't come right off the chain, I had panicked. Next time, yes, I'd know better. "We'll talk about that later. Right now, Ivan and I have an appointment with Kevin Tolley."

Zoe dropped the spoon in the carton. "Fine. Don't let

me keep you from your appointments. But I suggest you put that *thing* in the drawer."

"Triple T! Triple T!" Milo hadn't forgotten just yet.

"Team Triple T?" Ivan nodded and pointed to me.

"Yes, that's my team. What team are you on, Ivan?"

He grinned. "Team Tolley."

Okay, that narrowed it down to two. "What career are you interested in?"

"Journalism. Foreign Correspondent!"

Seemed perfect for him. *If* he could learn English a little better. "I have a book on journalism. I'll bring it to school for you."

"Thank you." Ivan shook his head. "Arcade. Amazing friend."

I smiled. "I'll be back in thirty minutes, Zoe." I walked out the door, shaky, with Ivan following, and with the Triple T token still around my neck. Because you never know when you might need to escape Tolley Town.

CHAPTER 21

Sticks & Bricks

Kevin Tolley led me and Ivan through his living room and out to the backyard of his brownstone. "So, I started thinking, 'Hey, who needs to go to one of those overpriced gyms to get in shape? I can make stuff out of junk.'" Kevin flashed a non-chipped-tooth grin, and I stared out toward the little patch of ground that was covered with junk. "I give you the Tolley Home Gym."

"Well, you weren't kidding there, Kev." I figured if I called him Kev he'd start to think of me as a friend. And kids don't usually punch out their friends. "This is . . . well, there are no words to describe what this all is. How about you tell me, uh . . . what it all is?"

Kevin walked down the back stairs to the junk, and Ivan and I followed. "This is circuit training, boys. And I call it 'Junk Fit.' Wanna give it a try? Do you work out?"

"Um, sure," I said, staring out at the tires, bricks, sticks, tarps, and tree stumps littering his backyard.

"I have never done . . . work out." It was the first almost full sentence I ever heard from Ivan.

"Well, you've come to the right place." Kevin walked straight to an area that had some broomsticks with milk cartons duct-taped to the ends. "Your legs are your strongest muscles, so we'll start with them. Arcade, grab that side of the barbell and we'll lift it up on Ivan's shoulders."

Ivan shook his head and began to walk away.

"It's okay, buddy, you can do this! The bar isn't that heavy, and Arcade and I will be your spotters." Kevin picked up his side of the barbell and set it down. Then he put his palms in the air. "It's light, see? Trust me, I'm an expert at this stuff. I won't give you more than you can handle at first. You're just a beginner."

What was *this*? Kevin Tolley being an encourager?

Ivan slowly walked back toward the barbell. Then he took off his sweatshirt to reveal skinny, white arms popping out from his short sleeve T-shirt.

Kevin grabbed the sweatshirt and draped it around Ivan's shoulders. "Here, this will add some padding. I've been looking for foam in the dumpster to wrap around this broomstick, but so far I've been skunked."

Dumpster diving for health and fitness. I'd never thought of that!

"Okay, Arcade, let's lift on three and put it on his shoulders. And make sure you let it down easy, so we make sure he can handle it."

I bent down and grabbed the milk jug.

"Okay," Kevin said. "On three. One . . . two . . . three!"

I lifted. It wasn't too heavy, but I didn't lift as quickly as

Kevin did, so we were a little off balance at first. But I got the thing up there. Ivan grabbed the broomstick with both hands.

"Keep hold of it for a minute, Arcade. You okay, Ivan?"

"Yah. Okay."

"Now even your hands out so you don't get tippy. We're gonna let go now. You'll be fine, though. This is the beginner bar."

Ivan moved his left hand out a little and smiled.

"Good! That's exactly right! Now, keep your weight centered, and slowly bend your knees, but don't go down very far just yet. Back straight. Look forward, but don't lean forward."

I wondered if Ivan understood all this.

Kevin grabbed an empty broomstick, put it on his shoulders, and stood across from Ivan, mirroring a perfect stance. "You feeling comfortable?"

"Yes, okay."

"Then let's do five half-squats. Here we go! Breathe in on your way down and breathe out on your way up."

I watched in amazement as Kevin Tolley led Ivan in his very first squat set. The kid could do this for a living. And this would make a really cool project for the career expo. What followed next was more instruction for Ivan, and a killer workout for me.

Kevin grabbed my bicep and pinched. "You seem beefy. I'm gonna give you the intermediate circuit."

"What? I thought we were going to talk about your project. I was thinking that you could . . ."

Kevin shook his head. "Not yet. First you need to do some brick burpees."

"Brick burpees?"

"Sure. Anyone can do *regular* burpees. Grab some bricks from the pile over there." I looked at the pile. There were all different sizes of bricks, and they had black numbers written on them. I went over and picked a pair with the number three. "Okay," Kevin said. "Now jump up with the bricks above your head. Then put the bricks on the ground, hold on, and kick your legs back. Do a pushup, get back up, and jump with the bricks in the air again."

Ivan was now sitting on a stack of old tires, breathing hard and wiping his neck with his sweatshirt.

"How many should I do?" I asked Kevin.

"As many as you can until you're sure you can't do anymore."

"Oh." That did not sound good.

"And then do three more after that."

I'd read about "the burn" in books, but after ten "brick burpees" I was experiencing it in real life. My Triple T token slammed against my chest each time I reached up with the bricks. This would have been a good time for glitter to pour down, but the only thing that poured was rivers of sweat down my back.

I began my eleventh burpee, and I got stuck down on the ground in the push-up position.

Kevin got down at my level and unleashed a barrage of not-so-empathetic commands. "Two more! Come on! Don't give up! Weakness is in the mind. You can do it, Arcade!"

Weakness sure felt like it was in my legs. And in my arms. And in my chest . . .

"Get UUUUUUP!" The bark from Kevin kind of scared me up. "NOW! TWO! MORE!" Kevin pulled a couple of number ten bricks from the pile, and he mirrored me, just like he had done with Ivan. "I'm gonna match you, and then we'll finish together." He pounded out eleven brick burpees in seconds. The dude was strong. And strangely motivating. "Okay, here we go, Arcade. Two more."

I can *do this.*

We both hit the ground, shot our feet out in back of us, and dropped our chests to the ground. Then, with a big grunt, I pushed myself back up.

"Yes! Go, friend!" Ivan cheered from his seated position on the tire.

"ONE MORE! NO PAIN, NO GAIN! GOOOOOOO!"

I hit the ground again. The rough edges of the bricks bit in to my hands as I threw my legs out behind me and dropped my chest.

"Now PUSH!" Kevin yelled.

So I pushed. And I bent my knees and prayed that they would lift me up. One. More. Time. They did. And I jumped with my hands in the air. One of the bricks flew out of my grip, fell to the ground, and broke in half. Then *I* fell to the ground. Thankfully, I stayed in one piece.

"YEAH! YEAH! YEAH! I knew you could do it!" Kevin jumped up and down, waving his arms like he had just won an Olympic gold medal. He jogged over to what looked like a rusted-out metal box in the corner of the yard, pulled on a handle, which opened a door, and he grabbed two cold water bottles. He handed one to both Ivan and me.

I could barely reach up for mine. "Thanks." I cracked open the cap and swigged half the bottle down.

"Staying hydrated is important," Kevin said.

I sat there on the ground, huffing and puffing. "Kevin, how do you know so much about working out?"

Kevin walked over to a humongous tire and started flipping it over, wearing a path beside the back fence. "Our family used to have a gym membership." Flip. "I asked the trainers a lot of questions." Flip. "Took their advice." Flip. He stopped and looked at me. "But then my dad lost his job and we had to cancel everything so they could afford to send Michael to the high school for smart kids."

"Oh, sorry about that."

Kevin shrugged and flipped the tire again. "Dad got another job, but he doesn't make as much money now. Fine with me. I got all I need here." Then he went over to another pile and grabbed a large tree branch. He pounded it into the tire like an axe.

I guess one man's junk is another man's sports gym. And *that* gave me an idea for his project. And I wouldn't have to trick him at all. Just trust the process.

Don't be so scared of striking out that you fail to swing.

"Kevin, what if your project was all about being a gym owner?"

Kevin smacked the tire with the branch again. "Nah. I hate business stuff. I'd rather just do the training."

Of course.

"Perfect! I'll go to the library and research exercises, and I'll write up some training plans for the kids for the career expo. And I'll design a display that includes some exercise equipment made of junk."

Kevin stopped pounding and wiped sweat from his forehead with the back of his hand. "But you don't know anything about this stuff. I saw how you do burpees."

I squeezed one of my tight biceps. "I tried hard, Kevin."

"You did. But you need to work on form. I'll fail the project if I let *you* come up with the stuff."

"But we have a deal, remember?" I winked and checked for Ivan's whereabouts. He was trying to jump rope with an old garden hose over by the tires. "I do your project, and you keep people from ripping me off."

"*I'd* be the one ripped off if I let you do this project. Tell you what, you help me find the books I need and help me write everything so it sounds good. But you can't come up with the ideas. Got it?" He punched me in my left arm.

Ouch!

I gritted my teeth. "Got it."

CHAPTER 22

Sore

"Ohhhhhhhh . . . Ow."

I flipped over to my other side in bed, but that wasn't any better.

"Uggggggh. I despise you, brick burpees!"

Thump, thump, thump.

"Arcade? Are you up? I heard you yell. Did you drop another book on your face?"

I wish. I had tried to read a book last night but couldn't lift it.

Thump, thump, thump.

"I'm coming, Zoe!" And I couldn't undress myself last night either. So, there I was, in my clothes again.

"Arcade, can I come in?"

"Yes, please."

Zoe cracked the door and peeked around. Then she opened it all the way and just stood there. "Hey." She didn't look like her normal bossy morning self.

"Hey. What's wrong? You're not dressed." That was not a tease. She really was still in her pajamas.

Zoe plodded in and sat on the foot of my bed. "I can't do it. I just can't." Then she started crying and her face fell into her hands.

Oh, ugh. A crying big sister is not a good thing. I flung back the covers and crawled, my whole body in pain, to the end of my bed. Then I collapsed on my stomach, with my face hanging over the foot of the bed.

"I've never been so sad in my entire life." Zoe sobbed. "I miss all my friends in Virginia. The kids here are so different, and I'm behind in all my subjects. Everyone seems to know more than me. None of the girls talk to me at school. I don't get it. What's *wrong* with me?"

Whoa. I had no idea Zoe was feeling like this. I'd been so wrapped up in my own stuff.

". . . and Mom and Dad are *never* here, so I can't talk to them . . . and you have that *weird token thing* going on, and yesterday I thought I lost you! Don't *ever* do that to me again, Arcade!" She pounded her fist on the mattress. "If we go through those doors again, promise me you'll come right back, as soon as the pulsing light starts. What if you hadn't come back yesterday? Who would I have in the world to tease and to laugh with and to take care of?"

I did my best to pull myself up to a sitting position. "I'm sorry, Zoe. I just wanted to see the home run."

"At the risk of losing *everything*? What good would it have been then?"

Zoe got up and pulled a tissue out of the box on my desk. She blew her nose and came back to sit by me.

"Arcade, would you pray for me? I really need God's

help to get through today."

I managed to roll off the bed and kneel next to it. Our family has always prayed together, but most of the time it's my parents praying for us kids. Could I do this?

"Sure." What else could I say? Zoe joined me on the floor.

I cleared my throat and closed my eyes. I felt Zoe's arm on my shoulders. I paused for a minute and prayed that God would help me pray.

"Dear Lord, please help Zoe today. I mean, help her every day. She's new at school. Well, we both are, and things are really weird, and we're scared and confused and . . . we miss our parents and our old life. It's not fun right now. Well, the token thing is kinda fun. But that's weird too. But I know you will protect us. You always have. We love you. Amen."

As soon as I said Amen, Zoe hit me on the back.

"Thanks. That's just what I needed."

I looked up. "Really?"

She sniffed. "Yeah. You just reminded me that God is on our side."

"I did? What did I say?"

Zoe blew her nose again. "You don't even know what you just prayed?"

"Not really. The words just came out."

Zoe grinned a little. "That's even *better.* The words must have come straight from God." Zoe looked at the clock on the wall. "We've got five minutes to get outta here, little brother. But don't worry, we're going to make it. And today is going to be great."

I watched her walk out the door. And I strained to stand.

Yes, today would be great.

Because I planned to leave the token in my underwear drawer.

CHAPTER 23

Bored, But Then . . .

It was the most boring Wednesday ever.

Until things caught on fire.

We had a substitute teacher, Mrs. Chapman—who talked much quieter than Mr. Dooley—but we watched an old science video first thing in the morning, and then wore our pencils out solving algebraic equations.

After lunch, things heated up a little.

"Mr. Dooley says that you have a competitive project going on." Mrs. Chapman read from a printed-out lesson plan. "You have time to work on it now, so get together with your teams and I'll be here at the desk if you need me."

What I really needed was a great career idea for my project.

Bailey was the first one over to my desk. She held a bunch of colored folders in one hand and a wad of matching highlighters in the other.

"I have finally figured out the perfect career for me." She took a huge breath and let it out. "Event Planner."

"Event?" I asked. "What kind of event?"

Bailey's eyes lit up and she shook like she had the chills. "Oh, anything, actually. Weddings, marathons, parades, stadium events . . . I *just love* planning things! My display will be how to plan a career expo! Isn't that clever?"

Doug and Amber scooted their chairs over.

"And, Doug," Bailey said, "I've been thinking about how much you love food."

Doug rubbed his belly. "I've been thinking about that too."

"Have you considered being a food entrepreneur?"

"Yeah, but I can't pronounce it."

"What? Entrepreneur?"

"Yeah, what you just said."

"Okay," Bailey sat down and passed out a different color highlighter to each of us. "Then how about just saying you are a food business owner. HEY—" She made us all jump. "How about owning a food truck business? They're super popular, and as an event planner, I would hire you for all of my events."

"Food *and* trucks?" Doug clapped his hands together. "Count me in."

Bailey dropped the rest of the highlighters on my desk. "This is going to be soooo fun! Dogs, food . . ." She looked at me. "So, what have *you* come up with, Arcade? With all those books you carry around, you must have compiled a grand list of possibilities."

Bailey leaned forward. So did Doug. Amber leaned in, but I think she suspected I had no list, because she had both hands over her mouth.

I sat up straight. "Uh . . . hmmmm." I pulled my backpack off my chair and unzipped it. Took out a couple of books. *Screenplay Writing: Ten Steps to Action!* and *The Alps and You: A Guide to Altitude and Adventure.* I stood them up on the desk with the covers facing toward my team members.

Bailey twirled her curly blonde hair with her pencil. "Sooo, do you want to write a movie or be a mountain climbing guide?"

Doug jumped up. "Or maybe he wants to write a movie *about* a mountain climbing guide."

Now Bailey was twirling her hair with the pencil *and* tapping her orange highlighter on the desk. "Both of those ideas are worth exploring. Which one appeals to you the most?"

"Well," I grabbed the Alps book and turned to the title page, "I've only read the first chapter in each of these."

"I could totally see you as a mountain climbing guide," Doug said. "I'd climb up a mountain with you! Any mountain! Doesn't matter how high."

Bailey sketched a picture that looked like a little hill. "Your display can include equipment necessary to climb mountains, and you could design and build a small mountain for the kids to try out."

Design and build? No, that's my dad's talent. And Casey's. I just wanted to know about the Alps. And possibly climb them one day. That is all.

Bailey turned her project booklet to the page where we're supposed to list all the team members' career choices. Then she wrote this:

Team Triple T Career Choices

Bailey (Team leader): Event Planner
Amber: K-9 Officer Trainer
Doug: Food Truck Entrepreneur
Arcade: Alps Mountain Climbing Guide

"This could work!" Bailey smiled. "The kids could come and play with a dog, climb a mountain, and then eat something yummy to celebrate. After that, I'll explain how the success was *all* in the planning."

"It has a lot of exciting elements." Amber gritted her teeth and glanced over at me. "Arcade, you're being very quiet."

I was frozen. Like the Alps in winter. Me? A mountain-climbing guide? That didn't make any sense at all!

In that instant, I changed from frozen to hot. Like the kind of hot that is under the surface, where you feel like you're going to explode if you don't get out of the situation you're in. Immediately.

"I'll be right back." I ran out of the room, toward the drinking fountain, where I downed about a gallon of water. Amber showed up while my chin was dripping on my shirt.

"Arcade! Are you okay? I told the teacher you were sick." She stared me down. "*Are* you sick?"

I wiped the water from my chin. "I don't know. I just feel hot. And restless. Like I have somewhere to go, but I'm not sure where."

Amber pointed to my shirt. "Maybe your token is ready to take you on another adventure."

I wiped some water drops from my collar. "I didn't

bring the token today. I left it at home in my, und . . . uh . . . drawer."

Amber crossed her arms and tapped a foot. "Mmmm-hmmm. That could be the problem. It's probably trying to direct you somewhere exciting, and now you can't go."

"Why do you think *that*?"

"Arcade, I've been through the doors, remember? Amber Lin, Doctor of Veterinary Medicine? Our little secret? Your token is something special. I don't know how or where you got it, but I don't think it belongs at home in a drawer."

"Excuse me, young people. Class is taking place in here." Mrs. Chapman tapped her pen on a clipboard. "Will you be joining us, Arcade, or do I need to give you a pass to go see the school nurse?"

My head felt a tiny bit cooler. "I'm coming in."

"Oh, good. Some kids were asking if you brought your suitcase full of books today. They want you to help them figure out what to do for their projects."

I was going to be of no help today. I had left "Daisy" at home too. With the token.

"And then I got all hot and ran out of the room," I told Zoe, as we climbed up our stairs after school.

"That's what happened to me today, too, when I overheard Trista telling her friends that I'm stuck up. I walked as fast as I could out of that hallway."

"Stuck up? You're the *least* stuck up person I know.

Annoying, maybe. But stuck up? What exactly does that mean, anyway?"

I put my key in the door and pushed it open. The piercing sound of the smoke alarm assaulted my eardrums.

"WHAT'S GOIN' ON NOW?"

Zoe dropped her backpack inside the door and pushed her fingers in her ears. She ran around the inside of the bottom story of our apartment. "I don't see any fire!"

"I'll check upstairs!" I started up, looking for smoke, but could see none. I could smell *something* cooking, though.

Zoe retrieved a fire extinguisher from the cupboard under the kitchen sink and pushed me up the stairs with it. "Hurry, Arcade!"

I took two steps at a time. Now I could see smoke, but I couldn't tell where it was coming from. "Should I call 9–1–1?"

"Yes!" The high-pitched beeping of the upstairs alarm almost drowned Zoe out.

I checked my back pocket for my phone. Guess I had left that at home today too. I ran into my room. It smelled like a barbeque. But it wasn't hotdogs or steak that was cooking.

"Zoe! In here!"

Zoe ran in after me. "What?"

I pointed to my dresser. Black smoke poured out from the cracks of my top drawer.

Zoe flung the drawer open and pulled the lever on the fire extinguisher. My room filled with a white cloud, and foam overloaded the drawer until it spilled out on the carpet.

Zoe unloaded the canister until the smoking stopped. The ear-piercing alarms ceased.

We both stood there like statues, staring at the drawer. Zoe put down the empty extinguisher and ran to the hallway closet. She brought back a towel and threw it at me. "Better start cleaning up. I'm not sure where Mom and Dad are, but we probably don't have much time."

I edged toward the drawer and peeked inside. Every pair of my underwear was burnt like the ends of a brisket. But the Triple T token sat in the middle of the ashes, gleaming, shinier than I had ever seen it.

Zoe put her hand on my shoulder. "Forget what I said before. Whatever you do, Arcade, *never* let that thing out of your sight again."

CHAPTER 24

Arcade Livingston: Alps Mountain Climbing Guide

The next couple of days were uneventful, even though I kept that token around my neck the whole time. I never planned to take it off again, even in the shower. But it didn't light up or heat up, and I wondered if it had unleashed all its fire power on my underwear.

All of us on Team Triple T continued to develop our outlines, education requirements, and display sketches for our career expo assignment. I visited the school library many times and searched for the perfect career to replace "Alps Mountain Climbing Guide" as my career choice, but nothing seemed to fit.

Ms. Weckles was working on Friday after school when I went in for one last ditch effort.

"Arcade Livingston! It's about time you came to see me here at the school library. It isn't as fancy as Ivy Park Public Library, but I have some great books. And a Beta named Baxter." Ms. Weckles gestured to the blue fish with the hanging tail, swimming back and forth, nosing the glass of the clear bowl.

"Hey, little guy. Do you have any idea what I should be when I grow up?"

"You *still* haven't decided? I think you've checked out all the career books in New York."

"And I want to thank you for those. My classmates have found them quite useful. I wish I was being graded on how much I'm helping them."

"Hey, how about professional golfer?" Ms. Weckles pointed to my Friday sock choice, green with golf balls all over.

That made me think of the old, run-down mini-golf place back in Virginia where Derek and I used to go to putt the ball around and play arcade games. It was fun, in a retro kinda way, but a real grumpy guy owned it. What *was* that guy's name?

"I've never swung a real golf club in my life," I said with a laugh. "But my project as it stands right now is Arcade Livingston, Alps Mountain Climbing Guide, and I've never climbed a mountain either."

"Oooh," Ms. Weckles put her hands up to her cheeks. "French Alps or Swiss Alps?"

"Swiss. If I'm going to be a professional climber, I might as well go for the highest ones, right?"

"When you open your climbing school, I will be your first student."

"Pssst."

I looked around.

"Pssst. Over here."

I turned. It was a Tolley. I couldn't see his teeth, so I wasn't sure which one. "I gotta go, Ms. Weckles."

She waved. "Happy travels, Arcade."

Wait. What did she just say?

"Psssssssssst!"

The Tolley twin held up a handful of papers and jetted over to a round table in the back corner of the school library.

I walked over slowly, watching to make sure no one spotted us together. "Hey."

"Hey." Tolley tapped on the paper stack. "Check this out."

I sat down and took a minute to read. The front page said *Sixth-grade Project. Career: Treehouse Designer and Builder,* and the next pages showed a layout for a deluxe treehouse, complete with zipline.

"This is great! I knew you could do it, Casey."

He ripped the papers out of my hands. "What are you *talking* about? This isn't mine. I found this in my backpack! I mean, Casey's. We got our backpacks mixed-up after lunch."

Gulp.

Kevin went on. "And what do you mean, 'I knew you could do it, *Casey*?' Did you have something to do with this?" He curled his hand into a fist, crumpling the papers. I grabbed them from him and smoothed them on the table.

"No. I didn't. But I knew about his project topic. I just wanted to encourage Casey. I want to help people, you know, like I helped you work on the first part of your project. How is that coming, by the way?"

Kevin narrowed his eyes. "Quit changing the subject."

"What *was* the subject?"

We stared at each other for a minute.

Come on, token. This would be a good time to heat up and bury this guy in glitter.

"Uh, yeah, well, I don't know. It's just, this thing Casey did is really good, and it makes me mad. I don't want to get beat by my brother."

"There's a way to make sure that doesn't happen."

"What? How?"

I pounded my fist on the stack of papers. "Just make sure yours is better. You have an amazing idea, Kevin. Think about it! Junk Fit? It's the coolest thing ever. You've got nothing to worry about."

"I don't?"

"No." I pointed a thumb in my direction. "Because I'm *doing it* for you, remember?"

Kevin shook his head. "Oh no you don't! If Casey could do his own, then I can do mine." He smacked his chest with his fist. "So don't mess with me, Arcade. You don't know anything when it comes to Junk Fit."

"Okay, you got me there."

It was quiet for a few seconds. Kevin flipped through the papers some more. "But could I ask you a favor?"

Do I dare say no?

"Sure. What is it?"

Kevin shrugged, and I was shocked to see him look a little embarrassed. "When I get my paper all written up, can you look at it for me? I'm not the best writer. I can't do it as good as Casey."

I grinned. "I'd love to help. You know that everyone isn't good at everything, right?"

Kevin laugh-grunted. "Huh, yeah. Like you stink at brick burpees."

"Yep. Exactly like that. But don't go around telling everyone, okay? And I won't tell anyone I helped you with your writing."

Kevin held up a fist. "You better not."

I held my hands up and leaned back. "Deal."

Kevin Tolley exited the library, looking determined. I think he was actually excited about his project. It could be a good one too. His talent for motivating people to work out was amazing! And Casey—*that* kid could build just about anything. I laughed as I realized that all three Tolleys were talented.

Talented Tolley Trio? Could that be what Triple T stood for?

Nah.

CHAPTER 25
Scratchy

You ever meet someone new and feel like you've known them forever? That's Scratchy.

The next day, on Saturday afternoon, he came revving down my street on his electric scooter, yelling out my name.

Dad sat up from reading the newspaper on the couch. "Arcade, someone's calling for you." He stood, went to the door, and opened it. "It's some red-headed kid. He's going the wrong way though." Dad chuckled. "You better go catch him."

Loopy and I had been hanging out on the living room floor. I pushed him off my lap and ran out the door.

"Hey, Scratch! I'm over here!" Scratchy had already zoomed a couple of doors past my house. When he saw me, he scratched his head, turned around, and pushed the scooter to the bottom of the brownstone's steps.

"RADICAL! I knew you lived on the Tolleys' street,

and if I yelled loud enough you'd come out. You wanna hang out? Go somewhere? Jump on!" He moved up a little on the scooter to make room.

"On that thing?"

"Yeah! Why not?"

I gulped. *I could be flung off that thing. Like a bull rider in a rodeo.*

"Okay. Can we go to the library?"

Scratchy scrunched up his face. "The library? Really? Why?"

"I have to return some books and get new ones. If I don't figure out a better thing to be for the career expo by Friday, I'll be stuck with Alps Mountain Climber Guide. I'm stressin'."

Scratchy parked his scooter and sat down on the bottom step. "Oh no! It's due *this* Friday? I haven't even started!"

"I thought you were going to bring in a car engine. By the way, where are you going to get a car engine?"

"My dad owns a shop, but I don't really know what I'm doing yet. I like to tinker, and I can fix most things." Scratchy laughed. "But not car engines."

Loopy had followed me out the door and jumped all over Scratchy.

"Hey, little rad dog!"

Scratchy picked him up and scratched Loopy under the chin.

"Feels good, doesn't it, boy? I hope you don't have dog eczema."

Scratchy put Loopy down.

"I'm down for going to the library if you still want to go."

I grabbed Loopy up. "Radical," I said with a smile. "I'll get my books."

I brought the daisy suitcase out and pulled it behind me and Scratchy on the electric scooter. I knew we looked ridiculous, but for some reason, with Scratchy it was cool. Kids on every street waved at us like we were in a parade. And when we rode past the subway entrance, I imagined glitter dropping and Scratchy and me flying through the doors, back to Virginia, so I could introduce my cool new friend to Derek.

But nothing happened. In fact, the token hadn't even heated up since the underwear burn.

I tried to talk to Scratch, but it was hard to hear with the high-pitched squealing of the scooter's motor.

"So, Scratchy, how do you like living in New York City?"

"I hate it!"

"Really? Why?"

Scratchy shrugged. "It's not home. I lived in Seattle my whole life. And then—*bam*—one day I'm here in the Big Apple getting sunburned. *Not* rad."

"Why did your family move here?"

"WHAT?"

"WHY DID YOUR FAMILY MOVE HERE?"

Scratchy turned off the motor and pulled the scooter off

the road. We landed right next to a hot dog stand. "You want a hot dog?" Scratchy dug in his pocket and pulled out a wad of dollar bills. "I'm buyin."

"Sure, thanks!"

Scratchy gave the hot dog guy the money, and the guy handed him two dogs. We stood next to the condiments, squirting on the mustard and relish.

Scratchy licked some spilled mustard off his arm. "You know how some kids can be real mean? Well, there were a bunch of kids bullying my big sister. She has trouble learning, and they just wouldn't let up. She came home sadder and sadder every day. It was awful. She's the sweetest person I know. This went on for a couple of years, and my parents finally decided to move across the country. My dad's brother lives here, so they run an auto shop together."

I suddenly lost my appetite. I thought about Zoe crying the other day, just having trouble fitting in, and how upsetting that was. I couldn't imagine what it would be like if she was being bullied every day for two years. "I'm real sorry about that, Scratch."

Scratchy looked me right in the eyes. "Thanks. She's doing okay now. The kids at her new school think she's rad. I figure that's worth me missing all my friends and the sunburn. You gonna eat that?" Scratchy pointed to my untouched hot dog. He had already downed his. I never thought I would meet a faster eater than Doug! I broke off half and gave it to him.

"Radical!" He shoved the whole thing in his mouth, chewed a couple times, and then swallowed.

"Whoa! Have you ever thought about being a competitive eater?"

Scratchy laughed. "Is that a thing?"

I jumped back on the scooter. "I think so. Let's check it out at the library."

I'm convinced Ms. Weckles lives at the library. "Hey, Arcade! What took you so long to get here? I pulled some more career books off the shelf for you." Sure enough, on the rolling cart were five books with a tag: *Hold for Arcade Livingston*.

I skimmed the titles. *Game Coding for the Clueless; CPAs Save the Day; Foundations in Floristry; Remarkable Marketing; Farming Families*. "These look great, Ms. Weckles. Thank you!"

"You are very welcome. I'll be back in five minutes and I'll help you find more."

Ms. Weckles took off—probably to grab a snack from her private kitchen in her secret library house.

Scratchy read the titles out loud. "Farming? That interests me. I like seeing something sprout up from nothing. You ever think about that, Arcade? How *different* things grow up out of the *same* dirt?"

"Yes! I HAVE wondered about that! And I *also* wonder how people figured out that goofy-looking things were food. Like coconuts. Did they just see one fall off a tree and think, 'Hey, let's crack that thing open and see what's in there?'"

Scratchy scratched his head. "I guess God could have told them what it was."

"Or maybe he had some fun watching them figure it out. Played a game with them. Find the fruit. Like with pineapples . . . and artichokes. Artichokes are the weirdest fruit. Or are they vegetables? How did they know just to eat the heart and the edges of the leaves?"

"And how did they know to put mayo on it?"

I scrunched up my face. "Mayo?"

"Yeah. What do *you* put on artichokes?"

"Butter."

"Butter?"

"Yeah."

Scratchy looked up toward the ceiling. "Huh, never thought of that."

I picked up the book on game coding and flipped through it. "Not sure I have the patience for this job, but it looks interesting." I put it back on the shelf. "I better return what's in my suitcase first before I check these out." I glanced toward the circulation desk to see if there was a line.

No line, but I did see something strange in the aquarium. It wasn't a fish. It was a face! Well, the face was on the other side of the aquarium, but I was sure it was looking right at me. "Scratchy, come here." I grabbed his sweatshirt sleeve and pulled him over behind the spinning fiction racks.

"You looking for a novel to read now?"

I put my finger to my lips. "Shhh. I think someone's watching us."

Scratchy peered through the metal racks. "Why would anyone want to watch *us*? Hardly anybody knows who we are."

My heart pounded in my chest. Just like it did when I was in that room with the old lady and the shadow. "I don't know. But that face in the aquarium gave me a bad feeling."

"My mom *always* says, go with your gut."

"My mom says that too."

"You think we should tell Ms. Weckles?"

I looked around, but I didn't see her anywhere. "I think we should just get outta here for now."

"Okay," Scratchy said. "I'll go grab your suitcase. Hey, where is your suitcase?"

I glanced back to the corner where I had left Daisy. She was gone.

Scratchy hit me on the shoulder. "Look!" he pointed toward the entrance to the library. A person wearing dark clothing and a ballcap was pulling Daisy out the door.

"Hey! You're taking my library books!" I yelled, and a bunch of people shushed me.

"Let's go get it!" Scratchy started toward the door.

I stopped him. "Wait! What if it's the face from the aquarium? And he's setting a trap for us?" My arms broke out in goosebumps.

"But he just stole a bunch of your stuff!" Scratchy put his hands on his hips and shook his head. Then he ran toward the entrance and walked a few steps out of the automatic doors.

I thought about all the "stuff" I had in the suitcase. Books. At least twenty! That would cost me a fortune in replacement fines. My library card was in there. And my project booklet. What else? I patted my back pocket.

My phone.

Scratchy ran back in, breathing hard. "It was an old guy. He just took off in a cab with your suitcase."

Chapter 26
Picking Daisies

"We gotta call the cops," Scratchy said. "That guy can't hide very long with a lime green, daisy-covered suitcase."

"Yeah, you're right." I ran up to the circulation desk. "Excuse me," I said to the unfamiliar lady who was checking out books. "There's been a theft. May I use the phone to call the police?"

"Oh no! A theft? What was stolen?"

Ms. Weckles appeared, and joined us at the desk. "What's wrong, boys?"

"Someone's been pickin' daisies!" Scratchy pointed out the door. "I saw him take off in a cab with all of Arcade's library books."

Ms. Weckles reached over the counter and picked up the phone, dialed a couple of numbers, and then handed the phone to me. "Speak slowly and clearly."

"9–1–1? What is your emergency?"

I took a deep breath. "Hello? My name is Arcade Livingston. I'm at the Ivy Park Public Library. Someone stole my . . . um . . . rolling suitcase full of library books. He also took my phone."

"When did this happen, exactly?"

"Just a few minutes ago. My friend ran out the door and saw an old guy getting into a cab with all my stuff."

"Okay, stay right where you are. We're sending a unit out. They'll be there in five minutes."

The police arrived in three minutes, and they were finished taking down their report in ten.

The officer made a quick call to someone and then pulled me aside. "We'll do all we can, Arcade, but I'm afraid the chance of finding your items is pretty slim."

I felt worse than if I'd been hit in the gut. "I'm going to owe the library for the rest of my life."

Ms. Weckles walked around to the other side of the circulation desk and began entering information into a computer. "Don't fret yet. I'm renewing all those books you have out, which will give you another three weeks to find them before any fines kick in."

"What about my phone?" I asked the police officer.

"It's probably been reset and sold by now. These thieves work fast. But, just in case, make sure your parents call your carrier and take it off your plan so they can't rack up any charges on your account. Would you like me to take you home and handle this with your parents?"

"No, it's okay. I'll let them know everything."

The officer looked concerned. "You sure?"

I nodded. "Yeah. I came here with my friend, and he can take me home."

"Name's Scratchy." Even Scratchy doesn't call himself Scranton anymore.

"Nice to meet you, Scratchy. Jerry Gerard, 20th precinct."

20th Precinct? I wonder if he knows Officer Frank and Samson.

"Nice to meet you, sir. Do you get many thefts from libraries? I mean, they can borrow the books for free, so why steal 'em? It's not reasonable."

Officer Gerard laughed. "That's a great question. Problem is, most criminals aren't reasonable. We never know exactly why they do things. Maybe the guy just needed a suitcase and didn't realize what was inside."

"Did you lose anything else, Arcade?" Ms. Weckles handed me a receipt for the renewals.

"Just my library card, and my project booklet from school. I can probably get another one. I hadn't really done much work in it with all the career confusion."

"And I can issue you a new library card. I'll even pay the replacement fee for you."

"Are you sure?"

"Of course. You're our best patron."

"Yeah, for three more weeks. After that, I'm toast."

CHAPTER 27

Breaking the News

Scratchy and I rode all the way home without talking. The motor squealed, and so did my head, with thoughts of what returning home without Daisy would mean.

I'll never be able to go to the library by myself again.

I'll never be able to check out books again.

I'll never be trusted with a phone again.

Mom will never lend me a girlie suitcase again. But that's okay.

We pulled up to our brownstone stairs, where Zoe was sitting, talking and laughing with Michael Tolley.

"Hello, Arcade." Michael stood and held out his hand to shake mine. I looked over at Zoe, and her cheeks had turned a little red.

"Hey, Michael."

"Who's your friend with the awesome scooter?"

Scratchy parked the scooter and came up the steps. "You can call me Scratchy."

"That's cool, Scratchy."

Zoe stood up next to Michael. "Michael was just telling me about his voice lessons. And he was singing a little."

The both looked at each other and giggled.

"Yeah, we've been having some fun. I'm trying to get your sister to sing with me, but she's a little stubborn."

"Zoe? Stubborn? Never."

"But Michael, you have such a good voice . . ."

They went on talking, like I wasn't standing there.

"I'm sure you do too, Zoe. Your speaking voice is lovely."

"Aww, thank you."

This was grossing me out.

"Zoe, I have to talk to you. Right now."

Zoe put a hand on my shoulder. "What's wrong?"

"Uh, there was a little mishap at the library," Scratchy said.

Michael stepped back. "Oh, hey man, I'm sorry. I'll let you two have some time." Then he turned to Zoe. "If there's anything I can do to help, just call me. You've got my number."

Zoe smiled. "Yes, I do. Thank you, Michael." She watched him as he walked across the street, and to his house, three doors down. Then she sat down on the stairs again. "So, what was this mishap that just interrupted my pleasant afternoon?"

Scratchy scratched the back of his neck. "I think maybe I should go. I'll see you on Monday, Arcade. Nice to meet you, Zoe." He walked back over to his scooter and revved it up.

I waved. "See ya, Scratch!"

When I turned around, Zoe was glaring at me. "Okay,

spill it." Then her eyes opened wide. "You used the token again, didn't you?"

"Use it? Zoe, I've told you, I don't even know how it works! I couldn't *use it* if I tried."

"Then what was the mishap?"

"Someone stole Mom's suitcase from the library. With all my library books in it. And my phone."

Zoe let her face drop in her hands. "What do you mean? Weren't you watching it?"

"Well, no. But who would steal a suitcase full of books? At a library? It's not reasonable."

Zoe sighed. "We're in the city now, Arcade! You have to be careful with your things. You have to *always* be watching . . . I should have been with you."

"Speaking of watching, I also think the guy who took the suitcase was watching us. I saw his face in the aquarium and it gave me the creeps."

"Did you call the police?"

"Of course. I'm not totally clueless."

"Good. Then let's go tell Mom. She's gonna hate that you lost Daisy."

"I didn't lose her, she was stolen!"

"Same thing."

Gulp. I wondered what it would be like to be grounded in New York.

We were about to walk in the door when Zoe's phone buzzed. "Arcade, why are *you* texting me?"

I raised my palms to the clouds. "My phone's stolen. I'm *not* texting you."

Zoe looked down at her phone. "Uh-oh." She turned it around to show me the messages.

I have your suitcase.
I will trade it for my token.
Details to follow.

"*His* token? What is he talking about? The token's mine. The lady gave it to *me*. My name is on it. How does *he* even know about it?"

"This complicates everything." Zoe sat on the floor in my room, where she had dragged me after seeing the text. She stared at her phone. "Should I block the number? Should I change *my* number? Arcade, whose numbers did you have programmed into your phone?"

That was easy to remember. "You, Mom, and Dad."

Are you sure that's all?"

"And Derek. Oh . . . and Amber, Bailey, and Doug. But I just added those on Friday."

"And do you have ICE information programmed in too?"

"ICE?"

"In Case of Emergency."

"Yes. Mom made me put in my address, phone, and other stuff."

Zoe hit her forehead. "Then he knows where we live."

"Not exactly. I programmed all that when we were still

in Virginia, and I didn't change it when we moved. So he *doesn't* know where we live."

Zoe blew out a breath. "And I don't think he can track my phone in any way. Whew. That's a relief. I'm going to block the number." She poked a few things on her phone. "There. That's the end of Mr. Suitcase Thief. We'll let the cops deal with him." She stood. "Come on, let's go tell Mom and Dad everything, except the part about the token for now. I have *no idea* how we would even start to explain that."

Mom and Dad were finally both home at the same time,. They sat on the loveseat in the living room, across from Zoe and me, where we sat on opposite edges of our couch.

". . . and the guy just ran out of the library, got in a cab, and disappeared." I felt tears well up. "I'm so sorry, Mom. I know how much you loved that suitcase."

Mom rushed over and wrapped her arms around me. "Listen, Arcade. I didn't love that suitcase, I love you. I'm so sorry this happened. I should have been there with you. I'm just glad you're safe. What a horrible experience this must have been for you."

I wondered if she could feel the chain with the token around my neck. Moms notice everything. I tried to pull back a little.

Dad came over, pulled Mom out of her hug, and gave me one too.

"I'm proud of you, son. You handled your first crime

in New York with courage and wisdom. Calling the police, filing the report . . . I would have been a mess if this had happened to me when I was eleven."

And here comes the grounding?

"We'll call the phone carrier, and then the police station to see if Officer Gerard needs any information from us. And then, I think we should have a family night."

"But don't you have to work?" Zoe asked.

"Yes, but I'm not going to. I think *Manhattan Doors* will open just fine without me tonight."

It was the best night we'd had in New York City yet. Dad and I threw a football in the backyard for an hour. Our yard isn't as big as the one we had in Virginia, but that didn't matter. We got to stand closer together and talk about everything—except the token. A couple of times, I *almost* told him. I hate holding anything back from my parents.

Zoe and Mom cooked up my favorite meal—spaghetti and meatballs. And since it was a warm spring night, we ate outside on our patio furniture, under an umbrella, in our new place. All together, like normal.

We played board games after that, and then we watched old movies of when Zoe and I were little kids. We laughed a lot. The next morning, we tried a new church in the city, and we sat together and worshiped as a family. The pastor talked about the storms of life, how God is our anchor, and how important family and friends are to help us while we are going through them.

It was just what I needed. Because I had a feeling a storm was coming.

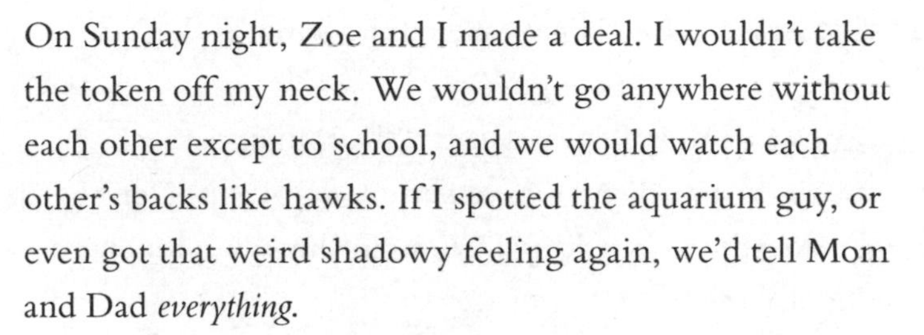

On Sunday night, Zoe and I made a deal. I wouldn't take the token off my neck. We wouldn't go anywhere without each other except to school, and we would watch each other's backs like hawks. If I spotted the aquarium guy, or even got that weird shadowy feeling again, we'd tell Mom and Dad *everything.*

Doug joined us for the walk to school on Monday morning. "I've been checking out food trucks," he said. "I can't decide what food I want to truck around. Ha! Get it? Truck around?"

I remembered the great spaghetti and meatballs from the night before. "I think Italian food would be good."

Doug rubbed his belly. "I think Italian food would be good."

"Or maybe a dessert truck," Zoe added. "With Belgian waffles."

"Hey, Zoe, did Belgian waffles originate in Belgium?"

Zoe threw her head back and rolled her eyes. "Stop, Arcade. Just stop."

"Well, if they didn't, I vote for warm chocolate chip cookies." My favorite.

"Warm chocolate chip cookies?" Doug licked his lips. "Where can I get some of those right now?"

"Yeah, I know. Let's change the subject." My stomach rumbled. "You're making me hungry."

Doug's phone chimed. "Uh-oh. Check this out! Event Planner Bailey has sent Team Triple T a message." He read, "*Don't forget—K-9 academy tour on Wednesday. **PUT IT IN YOUR PLANNER***. What's she talkin' about? I don't do *planners*. I'm a food truck guy."

Zoe came to Bailey's defense. "She sounds very thorough. You're lucky to have her on your team. Don't forget, Arcade, we're taking Milo in for his appointment on Wednesday too."

"Is that your bird?" Doug asked.

"Yes," Zoe said. "He has a little ailment."

"Yeah, I heard. Arcade told me he needs his beak wired shut so he can't talk."

Zoe gave me the stink-eye. "Did you tell him that?"

"Yeah, maybe. But that was right after we got here and all he would say was, 'Bawwwwk, New York, New York!' Like I needed a reminder that I wasn't in Virginia anymore."

As we approached the subway entrance, Zoe began to bite the nail on her pinkie finger.

I pulled her aside. "Don't worry. It's going to be a good day. They can't ignore you forever."

Zoe stared at me. "And the joke is . . . ?"

"No joke. You're a good person. They'll figure that out soon."

She smiled, reached out her hand, and pushed me back

a step. "Thanks. Now go *straight* to school, and don't go anywhere but here after it's all over. You got my back and I got yours, remember?"

"Yeah."

She turned.

"Hey, Zoe, you got something on your back."

She reached around and craned her neck to look. "What?"

"I dunno, but it's gross-looking. Oh, wait, that's just your blouse." I turned and ran with Doug.

I heard her yell, "And you have AQUARIUM BREATH!"

CHAPTER 28
Wednesday Weirdness

Wednesday came, and I didn't even have to put it in my planner. I would never forget about a chance to get rid of Milo. But I was also a little nervous, returning to the scene of the surgery.

Zoe met me at the subway entrance after school. We rushed home, got Milo, and then took the subway over to West 83rd Street, the location of the Pawsitive Pet Care Center.

"It feels different than last time," I said. "The building's the same, but it seems like it was on a different piece of property or something. The bushes and trees are smaller."

"And there's a whole lot less glitter." Zoe stood by the door, checking out the clouds.

"Bawwwk! Triple T! Triple T!"

"Milo, shhh!" Zoe carried Milo in a yellow bird carrier that looked like a backpack.

"Why don't we just drop the backpack at the door and run for our lives?"

Zoe grabbed the sleeve of my sweatshirt and held

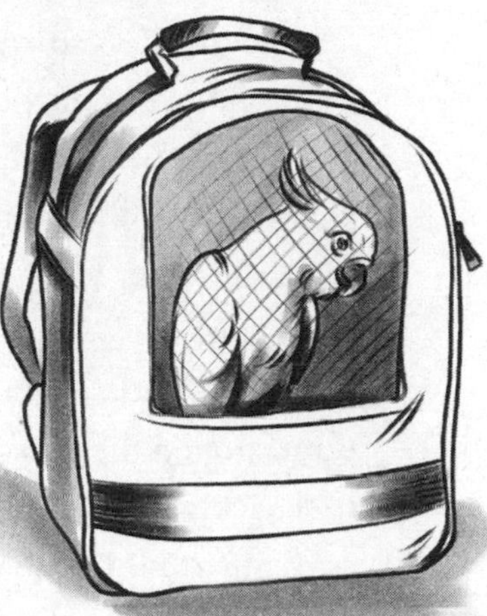

on tight. "Oh no, we're going in . . . together."

"But what if they recognize us?" I pulled my hood up over my head.

Zoe pulled it off. "You were a hairy man the last time you were here. That's highly unlikely."

"But you looked kind of like yourself," I reached over and flicked her ponytail.

Zoe sat Milo down on the ground, took her glasses out of her purse, and put them on. Then she changed her ponytail into a messy bun on the top of her head. "There, how's that?"

I covered my face with my hands and shivered. "Scary. But I think it will work."

"Okay." Zoe picked up Milo. "Be observant. Let's go."

Walking in the front door was the hardest part. I half-expected Kate to run up and pull us down the hallway to perform a cat appendectomy. But nothing like that happened. The office was full of pets—cats, dogs, birds, and there was even a little girl over in the corner with a pot-bellied pig.

"May I help you?" A dark-haired young woman greeted us at the front desk. She smiled. "Let me guess. Is this Milo?"

"Baaaawk! Triple T! Triple T!"

Be quiet, goofy bird!

"Aww, that's so cute! What is he saying?"

I pointed to the bird carrier. "You think *he's* cute? Ha!"

Zoe shoved her elbow in my side. "He's saying 'Dribble D.' We have this cousin, Derek, and he's a point guard, so that's our cheer for him. Dribble D." My sister is brilliant sometimes.

"Well, Milo is one smart birdy, if you ask me." The lady came around the desk to take a look at him through his little backpack window.

"Smart birdy! Smart birdy!"

"Yeah," I chuckled, "so brilliant he's pecking half his feathers off."

"Awww, he probably just needs a little medicine, right, Milo? I don't think your uncle likes you very much. What's your name, Uncle who doesn't like the smart birdy?"

"Me? His uncle? Nah, I'm not related. He can be annoying, so I like to tease him. My name's Arrr . . ."

Zoe gave me an intense stare.

"Arnie. Uncle Arnie."

"And what's your momma's name, birdy?"

"I'm Zoe."

"Okay, Zoe, would you and Arnie like to follow me back to the exam room?"

"Ummm, I'd like Arnie to stay in the waiting room. He stresses Milo out. He's probably the cause of the problem."

The girl laughed. "That's fine." Then she turned to me. "The waiting room is a little busy right now. We had a bunch of people walk in without appointments. You're welcome to sit in my chair until I return."

"Thanks, but I'm fine just standing right here."

"Okay. Zoe, you can follow me back."

Zoe gathered her things and whispered to me before she left. "Look around. But don't get caught." Then she disappeared down the clinic's hallway.

First, I went to the other side of the desk. It was the same desk as the other day, but now the block letter calendar said April 7th. A young woman wearing scrubs came in the front door, so I backed out of the space.

"Can I help you?" She breezed by me and grabbed a file off the desk.

"Just looking for some water."

She pointed to a mini-fridge in the corner. "We have some little bottles in there. Help yourself."

I flashed a grin. "Thanks."

She scanned the waiting room. "Wow, it's a busy one today." She disappeared down the hallway too.

I grabbed a bottle of water, loosened the top, and pretended to drink while I searched the walls for Amber's and my veterinary certificates. Didn't find them anywhere.

Whew. Okay, then maybe it was all just a dream. Or something like a dream.

A jingle sounded as some new people walked in the door.

It was a police officer with a familiar-looking, cone-wearing German Shepherd! The dog and I made eye-contact, and he began to bark and wag his tail.

The officer grinned at me. "Good afternoon. Samson likes you. That must mean you're a good guy." He reached down and petted him on the back. "He just had surgery a few days ago. This is the liveliest I've seen him since then."

I reached out to pet him. I could tell he knew who I was. Boy, was I glad he couldn't talk. "How's he doing? Is he your partner?"

Like I didn't know the answer to that.

"Yes." Frank peeked around at Samson's face in front of the cone. "He's my best friend too. He just can't keep himself from eating the wrong things."

I knelt down and let Samson lick my hand. "You gotta stop eating balls, okay, buddy?"

"How did you know he ate a ball?"

I stood up. "Oh, I . . . uh . . . just guessed. My dog Loopy eats balls. What else would a dog eat?"

"Oh, let me tell you! Socks, wallets, hats, sticks . . . I could go on. The ball almost killed him, though."

"How's he doing?" Sweat poured down my neck.

"He's healing nicely. The doctors here are excellent, right, Samson? We love Dr. O'Ryan. He had to take out some of his intestines, but he sewed him up real nice."

Dr. O'Ryan?

I glanced back up at the wall, and there is was. A veterinary certificate for a George O'Ryan.

Whew.

I turned back to Frank, who was waiting for me to respond to his last comment. What had he just said? Oh yeah, intestines. "Eight inches? That's a lot to take out. I'm glad it all went well."

Frank crunched his eyebrows together. "Did I say how many inches he took out?"

"What? Did you?"

"I don't know. Did I?"

It sounded like a conversation with Doug. Luckily, the dark-haired girl came down the hall and interrupted the awkwardness. "Hello, Officer Langdon. Doc said to bring Samson right on in."

"Thanks so much." He grinned at me. "It was nice talking to you."

"Nice talking to you too. And I hope Samson is one-hundred percent real soon."

Samson snuggled his cone right up to me. It scraped me in the knee. He licked and licked. Almost as much as Loopy.

Frank had to drag him away. "C'mon, boy." Then he looked at me. "Man, he *really* likes you."

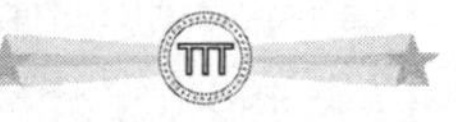

I sat next to Zoe on the subway and tried to talk her into taking me straight home.

"Whoa, that was a close call. I can't go to the K-9 academy after that. I'm too stressed. Someone's going to find me out."

She had her face up against the netting of Milo's carrier.

"Hear that, Milo? Your Uncle Arnie is stressed. Serves him right for causing your feather picking. Would you like to try Milo's herbal treatment, Arcade?"

It felt good to have Zoe tease me. Calmed me down, actually.

"Yes, we can go home. Do you want to text Bailey from my phone?" She handed it over to me.

"I would, but I don't have her number. It was programmed in *my* phone, which is gone. It was also written in my project workbook."

"Which is also gone," Zoe said.

Her phone buzzed in my hand. It was from an unidentified number. My temperature rose when I read it.

If you block me again, I will call your mom, the theif.

Zoe put Milo's cage down beside her. "What's up now?"

I showed Zoe, and she stared at the message without saying a thing for a few seconds. "Okay, let's think about this for a minute. He has *my* number, so blocking him will do no good. He'll just use another phone to contact me. But what does *this* mean, 'I will call your mom, the thief?' How is Mom a thief?"

"No, that's not how I read it. I think it means he'll call Mom. *Signed*, the thief, which is him. But he spelled thief wrong. I know the I before E thing is confusing, but doesn't he know that spelling is a very important skill?"

"The Babe said it himself," Zoe laughed and jostled

me with her elbow. "But commas are important too. The placement of this one is puzzling." She shrugged, then poked some things on the screen. "There, I blocked him."

"WHAT? WHY DID YOU DO THAT? Now he's gonna call Mom."

"So what? Let him. What's he going to tell her? I'm calling his bluff. He only has power if we give it to him."

I got goosebumps all over. "*What* did you just say?"

"Enemies only have power over us if we give it to them. Don't you see? He *wants* us to be scared. But *he's* the one who should be scared. He's the thief. And a bad speller at that."

I sat there, rumbling along with the subway car. My sister was right. "That's what the lady told me about the shadow, remember?"

"What? Are you talking about that day when you ended up in the park after us?"

"Yes. She said the same words you just said. 'He only has power if you give it to him.'"

Zoe nodded and smiled. "Smart lady. I hope I get to meet her someday."

CHAPTER 29

Undecided

Mr. Livingston, we are sorry, but that stop sign answer left us undecided. We need to ask you one more question in order to determine if you are the right person for the job."

"Okay, sure. Go ahead. I like questions."

"What do you want to be when you grow up?"

"Oh, uh . . . that's easy. Since I'm here, interviewing to be a sixth-grade teacher."

"We're waiting . . ."

"Yes, well, when I grow up, I'd like to be . . ."

"Do you need a few days to think about it?"

"No! It's Friday, April ninth. I have to decide today."

"Okay, then. Please tell us your answer."

"All right. Here goes. When I grow up, I'd like to be a . . . sixth-grade teacher?"

"Try again."

"A sixth-grade teacher."

"Try again."

"A sixth-grade teacher!"

Thump, Thump, Thump.

"Arcade! Are you up?"

"No! Try again!"

"What?"

Ugh. It was the morning I had been dreading. This time I woke up lying on my stomach, using a library book as a pillow. So glad I didn't drool.

"Hang on, Zoe." I walked over to my desk and skimmed over the paper I had typed up last night:

Career Expo Outline
Arcade Livingston: Alps Mountain Climbing Guide

Yawn.

Congratulations, Arcade. You have succeeded in presenting the job of Alps Mountain Climbing Guide as the most boring job on the planet!

"Someone's here to see you." The way Zoe sang that greeting made me want to throw myself under the covers. Who could it be? A girl? Or worse . . . a Tolley?

She opened the door a crack, and Loopy came through, his little body quivering with excitement. He jumped up in my arms and licked all the night sweat off my neck.

"Ha! Gotcha," Zoe said. "Had you worried there, didn't I? I thought you could use a little spit bath since you haven't bathed all month."

I picked up one of my scrap papers that I had folded into a plane and threw it at her. She knocked it down and stomped it flat. "Hey, it's Friday, so don't forget your socks!" She shut the door and I could hear her heavy feet thud down the stairs.

I fell down on the bed with Loopy still licking me. I couldn't help but be a little bit cheered up. "You wanna go to school for me today, Loop? You probably know what *you* wanna be when you grow up." I put him down, opened my bottom drawer, and pulled out a pair of navy blue socks with donuts all over them. "I know, you want to be a dog, right?"

Loopy stared at me and panted.

"You think Doug'll like these socks?" I pulled them on, then threw on some clean clothes. I grabbed my backpack, and Loopy and I headed downstairs.

"We have notes," Zoe said.

I grabbed Zoe's first and began a dramatic reading:

> *Dear Zoe,*
> *You amaze me. I can't believe how blessed I am to have you as a daughter. You make me proud every day of my life. Go out there today and dazzle them! You are God's treasure.*
>
> *Love, Dad*

I waltzed around the room with the note till I could hardly stand my own humor. I fell to the floor.

Zoe picked up *my* note and read it out loud:

Dear Weird Boy,
Get off the floor and quit bugging your amazing sister.
Love . . .

I yanked the note from her hands and read the real note to myself.

Dear Arcade,
The choices you're making today are shaping who you'll be in the future.
I'm proud of you.
Love, Dad

Zoe stood there, crossing her arms. "What, no dance?"

"Nah. Just confusion."

We got to school fast. Good thing, because all Doug did was talk about my socks, how much he loves donuts, and how he should add donuts as an option to his current chicken and waffles food truck idea. "See, it's like dinner and dessert all in one. Chicken *and* waffles. A donut's kinda like a waffle."

"Whatever you say, Doug."

We had to turn our outlines in before lunch. Mr. Dooley

said he wanted to grade them and return them before we were dismissed for the weekend.

"I EXPECT YOU TO START BUILDING YOUR DISPLAYS OVER THE WEEKEND. TIME IS TICKING, PEOPLE. THIS IS NOT THE ONLY SCHOOLWORK YOU HAVE, SO PLAN YOUR TIME ACCORDINGLY."

At 11:55, I slumped over to Mr. Dooley's desk and plopped my outline in the wooden box. Then I dragged myself back to my desk.

"It's going to be a great display, Arcade," Amber said. "Don't worry."

All I could think about was Dad's note.

The choices you make today . . .

Great. I'll be living in snow at the top of a mountain for the rest of my life.

"Did you hear the good news?" Amber was still trying to pop me out of my sorry mood. "I scheduled a K-9 unit to come to the career expo! Officer Brandon McCarthy and Cody, the German Shepherd. I'm excited, but I had really hoped for Frank and Samson. *If* they're real."

I started to tell her that they were, but the bell rang for lunch.

"OKAY PEOPLE. I HAVE PAPERS TO GRADE, SO IT'S TIME FOR YOU TO GOOOOOOOOOO!"

CHAPTER 30

Breathe

"Hey, Arcade! Over here!" Doug waved me over to the lunch table where he and the rest of our Triple T team sat. But at another table I spotted Ivan's coat, hanging on an empty chair next to him. I ran over to Doug.

"I'm gonna go sit by Ivan today. We good?"

Doug smiled. "Oh, yeah, we're good." He turned to the team. "He's gonna go sit by Ivan."

I took my tray over and set it down by the coat chair. "Can I sit here?" Ivan nodded and removed the coat.

On the other side of Ivan was Kevin Tolley. I knew it was him because when I sat down, he threw a napkin ball at my face. "Hey, Arcade. Ask Ivan to show you his muscles."

Ivan rolled back his sleeve and flexed. "Milk jug biceps."

I had to give it to Kevin and his Junk Fit Gym. Ivan's arms *did* look bigger than before.

"I made up a training schedule for Ivan, and he's been at my house every day workin' out. We're doin' before and after pictures with measurements to put in my Junk Fit Gym display. He's kinda like my fitness model."

"Do you like working out, Ivan?"

He nodded and smiled. "Hard, but good. I like."

Kevin threw *another* napkin ball at me. "And since Ivan has been helping me by being part of my fitness project, I've been helping him learn English."

I choked on my pizza. "Oh, well, that's a good thing, I hope."

"Yeah, it's always good to learn another language. He knows all kinds of words now. It's gonna help him one day when he's a foreign correspondent."

Maybe. I shuddered to think of what words might be part of Kevin Tolley's vocabulary.

"Kevin is friend," Ivan said. "Strong friend."

I smiled. "I'm glad. And your project sounds fantastic, Kevin."

"Yeah, now that I took it out of *your* hands, it's really coming together. You should drop by Junk Fit some afternoon. I can show you brick crunches next. That'll get you some rock-hard abs."

Ivan punched his stomach a few times. "Rocks!"

"Tell you what, Kevin, after the career expo, I'll take you up on that. But right now, my gut's all knotted up with stress."

"Stress? Why do *you* have stress?"

"I'm just nervous that my project isn't going to be good."

Wait. Why am I telling Kevin Tolley about my problems?

"This is what you gotta do, Arcade. Breathe in . . ." Kevin took a huge breath in and held it. Then he blew it out. "Breathe out the stress." He did it again. "See? Just like that. Breathing is important. I learned that while I was reading a workout book last night."

"You read a *book* last night?"

"Yeah, got it from Ms. Weckles. Stayed up real late trying to finish it. It's helping me with my career. I guess you could say you inspired me, Mr. Bookworm."

"Arcade is inspiration," Ivan said.

I breathed in. Held it. Then I blew out the stress. I finished my pizza with these strange new classmates. And, to my surprise, I did feel better. Until I got to class, where Mr. Dooley was handing back our outlines.

"I NEVER FAIL TO BE IMPRESSED BY SIXTH-GRADERS." Mr. Dooley beamed.

"YOUR OUTLINES ARE FANTASTIC. SOME OF YOU MAY HAVE TO SCALE BACK A BIT ON YOUR ELABORATE DISPLAY IDEAS, BUT I WILL LET YOU FIGURE THAT OUT. BE SURE TO CHECK THE GUIDEBOOK FOR YOUR SPACE REQUIREMENTS."

Space requirements? Uh-oh. That could eliminate a zipline.

"YOU CAN ALL COME UP AND GET YOUR OUTLINES."

I scooted my chair back and stood.

"MR. LIVINGSTON, MAY I HAVE A WORD WITH YOU? IN MY OFFICE?"

Mr. Dooley has a small office that's attached to our

classroom. He opened the door and stood there waiting for me.

Breathe in. Breathe out.

I trudged to the door.

"Hello, Arcade." For the first time since I'd been in his class, Mr. Dooley had dialed his voice volume down to two. I even had to lean in to hear him.

"Hello. Am I in trouble?"

He left the door to his office open but walked in and turned his back on the class. I had to face him, and unfortunately, I could see everyone over his shoulder. I pushed my glasses up on my nose.

Mr. Dooley crossed his arms and put one hand up to cradle his chin. "Tell me about the Alps."

I swallowed hard. "Well, there are the French Alps, and the Swiss Alps, and they're high mountains, and I've always wanted to climb them." I flashed some teeth.

"Tell me about being a mountain climbing guide."

"Um, well . . . sir, you have to really know the mountain to be able to guide others up it. And then there's special equipment you need, and training in how to handle medical emergencies and other . . . uh . . . things." More teeth.

The Tolley Twins were in my direct line of vision, and they were taking full advantage by making clown faces and flapping their arms around. I turned to the side to keep from laughing. Or crying.

Mr. Dooley handed me my outline. It didn't have a grade on it. "There's a lot of good information here, Arcade.

It's probably the best written paper in the class. No spelling errors, properly placed commas . . ."

Yes, that's important!

"But it's lacking passion."

"Passion?"

"Yes, passion. There's no excitement. No getting carried away. No dreaming here. You may have an interest in climbing the Alps once, but I don't sense you would want to spend your *life* climbing the Alps. Am I right?"

Breathe in. Breathe out.

"Yes, sir."

Mr. Dooley paced a couple of steps, then turned and retraced them. He stopped. "I tell you what I'm going to do. I'm going to issue you the 'New Kid Pass'."

"What's that?"

"It's something I just made up. It's going to buy you more time. I know you're in a tough transition. I moved across country when I was about your age, and it really threw me off my game for a while. I kinda lost myself while I was trying to adjust to new friends and a new school."

I felt my throat tighten. "Yeah, that's kinda how I feel."

Then Mr. Dooley got in my face a bit. Thankfully he blocked my view of the Tolleys. "I like you, Arcade. Everybody does. Even the bullies. That's a gift you have with people, you know that?"

"It is?"

"Yes. And there's a reason you're like that. You were made on purpose for a purpose."

"I was?"

"Yes. So were all the kids in my class. Now, I know a lot of them aren't going to actually end up doing the jobs they pick for their project, but that's not the reason for the project."

"It's not?"

"No! It's for you to think about who *you* are, deep down, right now, when you're eleven. It's for you to discover what gets you excited, what you're good at, and then realize that your unique gifts are valuable to this world."

I felt a weight lift. "Oh. That makes sense."

First thing to make sense since I got to New York.

Mr. Dooley took my outline from me, ripped it up, and threw it in the trash. "Start over. You can turn this in at the career expo. I'll be okay with whatever you choose to do, as long as it represents who *you* really are. Got it?"

I smiled. "Yeah. And thanks, Mr. Dooley."

Chapter 31
In the Pits

For the next three weeks, I dug in and researched careers harder than ever. Ms. Weckles could hardly keep up with my requests for books. Time was ticking, and I had to find a good job soon so I could start my display.

One Saturday morning at the end of April, when Zoe and I were hanging out at the Ivy Park Public Library, Ms. Weckles broke some bad news. "Arcade, we have a library policy that states if you have any overdue books, you can't check out any more."

Had three weeks gone by on those renewals already?

"I've already stretched the rules a bit by letting you check out more books than is allowed."

"I'm sorry, Ms. Weckles. I'll bring back everything I have. And I'll ask my parents to call the police and see if they've found anything."

"That will be fine." She placed a couple of new career books in front of me. "You can read all you want here in the library. And I'll try to dig up some more books for you at the school library. You don't have any overdues there."

Ms. Weckles, you are my favorite person in New York.

Right then, Doug came in. *To the library.* "Hey, Arcade!"

Everyone shushed him. He looked around and whispered, "Oh, sorry. The library. Right." Then he continued to talk to me, without whispering. "Scratchy's outside. We're goin' food truck tastin'! You wanna come? There's a food truck festival in Midtown, and I gotta try everything and decide what I'm gonna have in my food truck display. It's so cool, Arcade! I found this huge ole' box, and I'm painting it to look like a truck."

There was definite passion there. And I *was* hungry. I closed the book I was reading and put it on the rolling cart by Ms. Weckles' desk. "Sure, I wanna come. Let me check with my parents first." Then I spotted Zoe, who was browsing in the Young Adult Reader section. We had made a deal to stay with each other, and with that thief out there, I intended to keep her real close.

“Can Zoe come too? She’s a foodie and could give some great advice.”

“Sure! The more the merrier!”

“Shhhhh!”

I’m sure the library patrons were glad to see Doug walk out the door.

We met Scratchy outside. He was standing on his electric scooter.

“How are we supposed to keep up with you on that thing?” Zoe asked, jumping up on the back of it.

“I got it all figured out. Me and whoever is riding with me will scoot to each line faster. And then you all catch up, and we hand you the food.” Scratchy stepped off. “But for right now, I’ll put it in manual mode. I can also fold it up and take it on the subway.”

“To the food trucks!” Doug yelled, and we took off toward the subway entrance.

“Zoe, you got any money?”

“I’ve got five bucks. That should get us through half a food truck.”

“No worries, I got us *all* covered.” Scratchy reached in his jeans pocket and pulled out a wad of cash. “I just got paid for a job.”

Doug's eyes widened. "You just got paid for a job? What kinda job you got, Scratch?"

Scratchy reached down to pick up some coins that fell on the floor of the subway car. "Fixin' stuff. My dad lets me work in the shop sometimes, and he pays me a little. This money's from installing my neighbor's new garbage disposal."

"How do you know what you're doing?" I knew Scratchy was mechanical, but he was only eleven.

Scratchy shrugged. "I just do. Plus, I've been takin' things apart ever since I was little. You know, to see how things work. Once I took off the front of the dishwasher. Mom wasn't too happy about that. But now I can install 'em."

I'm pretty sure my mouth was hanging open, finding out about this mechanical genius. "I've never thought to take things apart."

"I guess that's just how I was made." Scratchy smiled. "I can't wait till I learn a little more about cars, though. Heehee—I might get in real trouble if I take our family ride apart."

I laughed. "Yeah, wouldn't make sense to do that." Then I broke out in sweat all over my head. "Hey, Zoe, can you move over? It's getting hot in here."

"Hot? What's wrong with you? It's freezing on this car." Then she looked over at me and frowned. "Oh no. I thought that thing was broken."

"What are you talking about?"

She pointed to my chest. "Check it out, Mr. Happy Travels."

No wonder I was hot. My token was blazing and shining like a headlight beam through my shirt.

Doug put both arms out to the side, like he was trying to stop any of us from getting out of our seats. "Fasten your seatbelts, friends, we may be heading back to *The Munch*."

Scratchy scratched the side of his cheek. "What's *The Munch*?"

"It's a TV show," Doug said. "And I was on it! At least I think I was. Until I was rudely interrupted while mixing up a white chocolate raspberry wedding cake."

Zoe rolled her eyes. "Hey, Mr. No Table Manners, we saved you from being embarrassed on national TV."

"Huh?" Scratchy looked totally confused.

I stood and grabbed one of the poles to stabilize myself. Sweat dripped down my neck. Followed by glitter.

Zoe packed in close to me. "I can't believe we're doing this again."

Scratchy stood and grabbed the same pole as me. "What? What are we doing? Why is glitter falling on us? Where's it even coming from?"

I didn't have time to explain. A set of doors appeared in front of the subway doors. The coin slot popped out of the middle and pulsed, and this time a sign appeared above the doors!

JOB SPEEDWAY

Scratchy pointed to the sign. "Hey! How does the subway know my team name?" Then he began scratching his ears. "WHERE is all this glitter coming from?"

I looked over at Zoe. "Job Speedway? Well, at least we have a clue this time. What should we do, sis?"

Zoe put her hand on her chest. "Wait, you're ASKING me what to do? That's a first."

I smirked. "Yeah. But I don't guarantee I'll take your advice."

"Fine, shark bait. Put the token in. But remember, this time my name is Zoe. Not Zoo!" She linked her arm with mine.

Scratchy stepped forward to examine the doors and the coin slot.

"Check this out," I said.

"Check this out!" Doug moved in closer.

"Job Speedway, here we come!" I pulled on the token and it popped off the chain. I reached out and dropped it in the slot.

"All clear," a subway voice said over the loudspeaker.

"All clear!" Doug yelled.

I made the door-parting motion with my hands. The doors made a dinging sound and they opened.

Gasoline fumes assault my senses, and I can hardly hear a thing over the roaring of race car engines. We're standing on a wall. All . . . five of us?

Me. Zoe. Scratchy. Doug. And the old lady from the library! She's wearing the Triple T ballcap and is holding a metal car jack that is bigger than she is.

Scratchy's standing on the wall to my right, steadying a bulky tire. And he's looking kind of bulky himself. And older. And very confused. "AAAAARRRRCCCAAAAADE? Are we on a PIT CREW? For REAL? I watch this on TV *all the time!*" He looks around. "I think we're the rear wheel team!

Pit crew? Rear wheel . . . whaaaaaat?

We're all wearing matching orange uniforms with golden tokens on them. I read Scratchy's name patch. It says *Crew Chief Scranton.* I point to the patch with my free hand. "Looks like you're a little more than that, Scratchy."

He looks down. "RADICAL!" Then he yells out to all of us. "OKAY, I KNOW WHAT THIS MEANS! WE GOTTA BE FAST, PEOPLE!"

I glance to my left and see Doug, the one with the sideburns, holding a tire of his own on the wall. On the other side of him is Zoe, who is also looking more mature, but still has her hair in a ponytail, and is gripping what looks like a supersonic water soaker attached to a hose. She's staring at the racetrack. Doug's yelling at me, I think, but I can't hear a word over the thunderous roar of the crowd and the car engines.

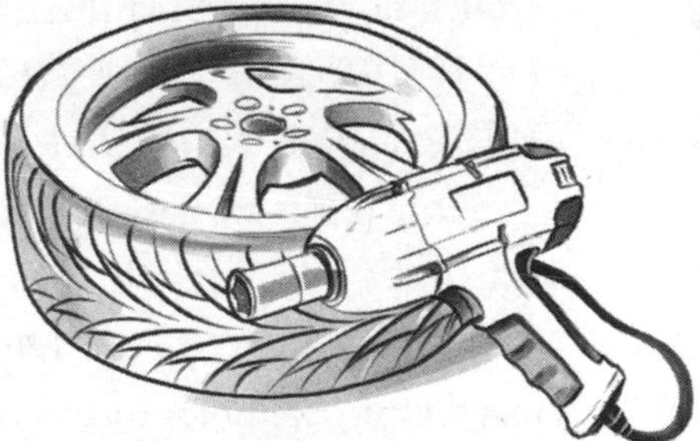

Scratchy hits me on the shoulder to get my attention. "You know how to use that impact wrench, Arcade? Remember, righty-tighty, lefty-loosey!"

I'm holding a supersonic water soaker too. Only it's called an *impact wrench.* I try to stop myself from hyperventilating so I don't get dizzy, fall off the wall, and get plowed over by a race car.

Calm down, Arcade. You've read a book about this. ***NASCAR*** *pit crews change the tires and refuel the cars during races, all in under 12 seconds! You're the rear tire changer. You pull the trigger on the wrench. It roars and turns left. That will get the lug nuts off.*

"WAIT!" I scream. "AM I SUPPOSED TO REMOVE LUG NUTS FROM A RACE CAR?"

Scratchy grins at me and tips his chin up. "Yeah, buddy! And don't forget to put 'em back on!" Then he looks around. "Who's our gas man?"

"He has all the fuel he needs," the mysterious Triple T woman says. "He just needs to keep his foot on the pedal."

Scratchy nods and then he picks up the tire. "Crew! Here's our car! PS 23! Let's get ready to roll!"

An orange stockcar with a PS 23 on it pulls into pit road. As soon as it crosses our line, we all jump to the ground. Scratchy and I run around the back of the car, over to the right rear tire. The old lady shoves the jack under the car and, somehow, she cranks it up so the car tips to the left. I crouch down and hit all five lug nuts with my wrench.

WHIRRRRRRR! WHIRRRRRRR! WHIRRRRRRR! WHIRRRRRRR! WHIRRRRRRR!

One of them flies off and smacks me in the chest, right where the token usually hangs. "OUCH!"

"ATTA BOY, ARCADE!" Scratchy lifts the tire up and matches up the holes to the wheel studs like he's been doing this his whole life. "Now, put 'em back on!"

I change the direction of the wrench and pull the trigger.

My shirt is already drenched in sweat from five seconds of pit crew work.

WHIRRRRRRRR! WHIRRRRRRRR! WHIRRRRRRRR! WHIRRRRRRRR! WHIRRRRRRRR!

Scratchy hits me on the back. "Okay, OTHER SIDE!"

Before I get to the left side, the old lady is already there, jacking up the car! "Teamwork is important," she says, but I hear her voice inside my head instead of it coming from her mouth.

"Who *are* you?" I ask, but I can't wait for her answer, because it's time to use the wrench again.

WHIRRRRRRR! WHIRRRRRRRR! WHIRRRRRRRR! WHIRRRRRRRR! WHIRRRRRRRRR!

This time, a lug nut hits me on the chin!

"OUUUUUUUUCH!"

But I can't rub out the pain. The clock is ticking. Five lug nuts need to go back on. Righty-tighty! I take a deep breath and pull the trigger.

WHIRRRRRRRR! WHIRRRRRRRR! WHIRRRRRRRR! WHIRRRRRRRR! WHIRRRRRRRR!

And as soon as I'm done, the car hits the ground and tears out of the pit.

"ELEVEN SECONDS! WHAT A RUSH!" Scratchy jumps up and down, high-fiving all of our crew. Except for the old lady, who has vanished. "Grab a tire, Arcade! We get to do this again in a few laps!"

Scratchy looks like the happiest guy in the universe. I, however, am shaking all over and don't know if I have the legs to change another tire. Thankfully I don't have to.

Golden glitter begins to fall, and the doors return on top of the wall. We step up. The coin slot pulses. I reach for my chain, and the token is there.

"Do we have to leave NOW?" Scratchy asks. "This is the most exciting thing I've EVER done! Can't we wait to see if we win the race?"

I shake my head. I hate to disappoint my new friend, but I learned my lesson at the baseball stadium. "I'm sorry, but we gotta obey the token. But don't worry, we'll win."

"How do you know?" Scratchy is brushing glitter off his shoulders and looks me right in the eyes.

I grin. "Because we have the best crew chief."

I pull the token off the chain, and this time, just to see what happens, I flip it with my thumb up in the air. It turns over and over—heads, then tails—glistening. Then it tumbles down, its golden edge lining up perfectly with the coin slot. It slips through. I make the parting motion with my hand, and we step off the wall together—as a team.

"What?!?" Doug asks in total awe. "Were we just at NASCAR? What were we doin' at NASCAR?"

We were back in the subway on our way to the food trucks.

I pulled the token out from under my shirt and let it dangle so my friends could see. "The token took us there. I'm not sure why, though."

Scratchy still had this huge grin on his face. "I don't know what that just was, Arcade, but it was the most RADICAL thing ever."

"I thought that thing was broken," Zoe said.

"I thought it was too. I guess it recharged."

"Is that some kind of magic time travel device?" Scratchy asked.

Doug gestured wildly. "It's MORE than that, Scratchy. Arcade's got some crazy power given to him by the library! Man, all I got from the library was some candy!"

All I could do was laugh. "I got this from an old lady at the library. She told me it belonged to me and then wished me happy travels. She was the jack operator on our pit crew. You all saw her."

They all stared and shook their heads.

"Oh, come on! You didn't see her? Then who do you think was operating the jack?"

Zoe put her hand to her chin. "It was that burly guy named Jack."

Doug nodded. "It was that burly guy named Jack!"

Scratchy scratched the back of his neck. "Yeah, I thought it was pretty funny, but that's what his name patch said. Jack."

My palms got all sweaty. "And I suppose you saw a gas man too?"

"No gas man," Scratchy said. "Jack said the driver had plenty of fuel, which didn't make sense to me, but we didn't have time to do anything about it."

Silence.

Zoe reached over and put her hand on my shoulder. "Are you all right, Arcade? Did you see the shadow again?"

I sat down. "Not this time. I'm fine, though. It was a fun adventure and all. I just wish someone else could see the old lady who gave me the token. That would help me know I'm not going crazy." I pulled the token up with the chain and flicked it with my finger. "I mean, *am I* going crazy? Is this real?"

Scratchy scratched the back of his neck and sniffed his palms. "It was real. I can still smell rubber."

Doug sniffed his too. "That was hard work. I *never* want to be on a pit crew again."

Scratchy leaned back in his seat and grinned. "I do."

Doug rubbed his belly. "Man, I'm starved! When is this subway gonna get to Midtown? Can your magic token get us to Midtown, Arcade?"

Right then, the subway car came to a stop.

"Midtown," Zoe said. "Are you all ready for an after-race snack?"

The subway dumped us out in a food lover's paradise. Trucks were lined up so close to each other that we didn't need the scooter. We just needed bigger stomachs.

"Dessert first! It's what my Gram always says." Doug pointed to an ice cream sandwich truck and we all headed in that direction. No complaints from me. Warm chocolate chip cookies with cookie dough ice cream in the middle? Yum.

"Lobster grilled cheese? Now *that* sounds heavenly." Zoe

studied the sign on the popular food truck. "A little pricey, though."

"Let's share one," Scratchy walked up, ordered a sandwich, and asked for it to be cut in four pieces.

Zoe ate hers faster than all of us and licked every speck off her fingers. "I'm going to save up and come get my own next time. *C'est délicieux*!"

"What's a Kati Roll?" That was the next food truck stop.

"It's like an Indian burrito," the woman inside told me. "Once you try one, you'll be hooked."

She was right. I don't know what all the ingredients were, but it woke up all my taste buds, in a good way. I grabbed my belly. "I'm getting full. Can we take a rest?"

"Right after the Belgian waffle," Doug said. "Or, hey, maybe I should get a thin crust pizza instead." He took off.

"This is fun." Zoe stopped to take a sip out of a water bottle. "I never saw this many food trucks in one place in Virginia."

Just hearing the word Virginia sent me to a sad place, and I realized that I hadn't called Derek in a while. I sure had a lot to tell him! Too bad I didn't have my phone. "I'm gonna sit this round out." I plopped down on a bench, and Zoe joined me.

Scratchy came over too. "You okay?"

"I think so. Just missing home . . . Virginia. Me and Zoe being here just doesn't make sense to me sometimes."

"I know what you mean. I've been here almost nine months now and it still feels weird." Scratchy sat down next to me and ate his waffle in silence.

I felt a bit of heat on my chest. I pounded it with my fist.

Must be heartburn.

A few minutes later, Doug returned with a thin crust pizza in one hand and his phone in the other.

"Hey, guys, my gram is sick and I gotta go take care of her right away."

"But you're right in the middle of project research," I said. "Can't your parents help out?"

"Nah. It's just me and Gram. My parents aren't in the picture right now. She's all I've got."

I had *never* talked to Doug about his parents. I had never met them, but I assumed they were just busy, like mine. "Oh man, I'm sorry, Doug. I didn't know."

He sat down, squeezing onto the bench with us. "I don't like to talk about it much. It's kinda painful."

I put my hand on his shoulder. "It's okay. You've got us too. There are a lot of things about life that don't make sense."

"You got that right."

And right when he said that, my heartburn got a lot worse. I grabbed my chest. It was hot. But *not* from the inside.

Zoe jumped off the bench and faced me. "I don't think so! It's too soon!"

I stood up. "What's too soon?"

"What are you two talking about?" Doug looked up.

And then his pizza was sprinkled with a new topping.

Glitter.

And a new food truck appeared, right in front of our bench. With elevator doors and a shiny coin slot.

"What kind of food is *this?*" Doug dropped his pizza to the ground.

I pulled the token out of my shirt. "I'm not sure. Are you guys up for trying something new?"

Scratchy and Doug said it together. "Totally!"

I grabbed the blazing token and it popped right off the chain. I glanced over at Zoe.

"I got your back," she said.

"And I got yours."

I threw the token in and made the parting motion with my hands. The food truck doors opened. "Let's do this thing!" I yelled, and we all stepped in.

CHAPTER 32

A Higher Perspective

We're not at a food truck festival anymore. We're in a small plane, flying high over New York City.

I can see the Statue of Liberty far below us—a tiny, white speck.

"Dude! I hate heights!" Doug pokes his head in between me and Scratchy, who is flying the plane.

WAIT. Scratchy is flying the plane?!?

"How long you been flying planes, Scratch?" Doug grabs his throat and plasters his face to his window.

Scratchy fiddles with some levers on the instrument panel. "Uh . . . I *don't* fly planes. Do you see a nametag on my shirt that says Pilot Scranton?" Then he turns to me. "Do you fly planes, Arcade? 'Cause we're IN A PLANE that is actually flying."

Zoe is sitting behind me. She kicks my seat. "My phone screen is all glittery again."

Scratchy picks up something from the instrument panel that looks like a plastic cup attached to the end of a string. No, that's *exactly* what it is. He speaks into the cup. "Hello?

JFK? Newark?" He turns to me. "What's that other airport with the funny name?"

"I don't know. I'm new here, remember?"

He continues to talk in the cup. "This is Thomas Scranton, and I'm flying a plane."

"That's your name?" I chuckled. "Thomas?"

"Only when I'm flying a plane." He puts his mouth in the cup. "Hello?"

A voice comes back. "This is Newark. We copy, Scranton. And by the way, you are talking into a cup. Try the radio."

"I don't know where the radio is."

"Try some switches. One of them will be the radio."

"Okay." Scratchy hands me the cup and begins throwing switches.

The first switch is not a good choice. The left wing dips, and we all lean far left.

My head smashes into Scratchy's neck. "AHHHHH! Switch it back!"

He does, and we dip right.

"AHHHHHH!" He puts the switch back to the middle and scratches his head. "Well, that's not how a plane should work."

"We're communicating through a *plastic cup*," Zoe says. "This is probably *not* your average plane."

"Uh, hello? Newark? 10–4? Anybody there?"

"Yeah, we're here, Scranton. We see you dipping all over the place. What a bunch of amateurs."

I grab the cup from Scratchy. "That's cause we're only eleven!"

"Excuse me?" Zoe taps me on the shoulder. "*I'm* fourteen."

Scratchy takes the cup back. "Newark, can you tell us what to do right now? And how we're supposed to land this thing?"

A few laughs come through the cup. "You can't even keep the plane straight! What makes you think you can land it?"

Great. We have a bunch of comedians in air traffic control.

"Scranton and friends, why don't you just sit back and enjoy the flight? Take a look around? Get a new perspective?"

"O-kay," Scratchy leans back in his seat. "You heard him, people, take a look around."

So we do.

And it really is an *amazing* sight. Manhattan looks so small from up here, like towers built out of floating toy blocks, with water all around.

"Wow, this is where we *live* now, Arcade." I look back at Zoe. She has her hand over her mouth and tears are forming.

I point to some blue rectangles on top of the blocks. "Are those pools on the roofs of the buildings? We need to find us a pool."

"Scranton, we're going on a break. We'll be back in a few to check on you. Copy out."

"Copy out?" I take the cup from Scratchy and tap it on my knee. "Are you allowed to copy out? Helloooooo?"

Scratchy holds both hands up. "I'm not touching nothin'. I think we should just sit back, like they said. New

York's a lot different from way up here. Cooler than from the ground. Don't ya think?"

We all sit back, stunned. No sound. Just the propellers humming.

Doug passes something up to me. "You want a hot dog? There's a bunch of 'em back here."

"Why not?" I grab one and take a bite.

"Hey, guys, look! It's Central Park. And there's the Upper West Side. I wonder if we'll be able to see our house, Arcade." Zoe aims her camera and takes a picture. She tries to look at it on her phone. "Glitter. That's *all* I get!"

I look out the window and realize we are dangerously close to the ground. "Scratchy, did you push something?"

His hands are resting behind his head. "Nope. But check out this switch. It's pointed to Window Magnification Mode. So that's what I think's goin' on, I bet. I didn't know planes had Window Magnification Mode."

Doug munches away in the back. "This is the *best* hot dog I've ever had! Maybe I should go into the airline food business."

Zoe hits me in the shoulder. "Arcade, check it out! There's Daisy!"

"Daisy?" Doug burps. "Who's that?"

I peer out my magnification window in the direction that Zoe is pointing. There, pushed into a bush in Central Park, is Mom's lime green suitcase.

Zoe tries to take another picture. "Glitter. That's all I *ever* get now."

I stare at the scene out the window. I could retrieve that

suitcase today, return the books, and not incur a single fine! If the books are still in it. And *if* we ever get down from this crazy plane ride.

"Scranton, this is Newark. We're back."

The voice fills the whole cabin now.

"It's about time," I say. "Are you going to bring us down?"

"That depends, Arcade. Do you want to come down?"

Traffic control knows my name.

"Of course I want to come down!"

"Why? All you've done is complain ever since you got to New York."

"Who are you? Is this a trick question? Because I'm not real good at answering . . ."

The plane sputters and dips.

"Rats!" Doug yells. "Mustard all over my shorts!"

"That'll *never* come out," Zoe says.

"Um, Arcade? I think we're running out of fuel." Scratchy points to an LED display that scrolls the words YES . . . YOU ARE RUNNING OUT OF FUEL . . .

Newark speaks again. "Scranton, we're going to turn your plane around."

The plane makes a left U-turn so tight we all whip to the right. It continues to sputter, and then the nose drops. We pick up speed and head toward water.

"AHHHHHHHHHH!"

"Calm down," Newark says. "Remember, you're on Magnification Mode. Objects appear closer than they are."

"But we're still FALLING!" I yell back.

"No, you're *descending.* That's how planes land. So make

sure your items are stowed appropriately, and your seats are in the upright position . . ."

"AHHHHHHHH!"

"And you still have to tell us *why* you want to come down."

"Tell him, Arcade! And hurry up!" Scratchy is leaning back and white-knuckling the arms of his seat.

"Ummm, okay, well, I want to come down because . . ."

KERPLUNK!

"What was THAT?"

"Scranton, give Arcade the cup."

Scratchy pulls on the string and swings the cup over to me.

I put the cup to my ear.

"That was the wheels coming down. You are running out of time."

I put the cup to my mouth, and I yell with all my might. "I want to come down so I can go home!"

"And where is home, exactly?"

I sighed. "New York. My new home is in New York City. And I want to be there more than anything. Safe and sound. With my family and my new friends."

The plane's nose rises, and then dips, like a dolphin jumping up out of the ocean and diving back in. Only that motion doesn't work well for people in planes.

I feel a weight hit me in the chest. I reach down, and there's the token. The instrument panel comes alive with blinking, multicolored lights—a lot like the video games at that old arcade where Derek and I used to play. It's also making plinking sounds like a pinball machine.

"RADICAL!" Scratchy yells.

A golden coin slot pops out right in front of me. And the LED display scrolls . . . INSERT TOKEN TO LAND . . .

"Are you ready?" I look around at my sister and my friends. "'Cause we doin' this!!!"

I pull on the token, and it comes off in my hand. I barely let go with my fingers, and it finds its way home.

And so do I.

CHAPTER 33

Lost in Central Park

"It's got to be around here somewhere, Zoe. That image is burned in my brain."

On Sunday, after church, we talked my mom and dad into taking us for a little stroll in Central Park. Loopy came along too. My parents rested on a bench and ate ice cream cones while Zoe and I went to check out some bushes. I tried to use Loopy as a "sniff and search" dog by letting him smell a book from Ivy Park Library. "Okay, boy, go find it!"

He just stared at me and panted.

"I don't know, Arcade. The park is really big. Everything looked much simpler from up above. This may not be the exact location. Or maybe he moved the suitcase since yesterday. Or maybe we really didn't see the suitcase at all."

Right then a text came through on Zoe's phone. She read it, then looked around frantically.

"What is it, Zoe?"

She held the phone out. It was an unfamiliar number, but from a familiar sender.

You think you can find it that easy?
We'll make the exchange at the career expo.
Three more weeks.

A bit of heat radiated from the token. I knew just what to do. “Give me that,” I said to Zoe, and she gave me the phone. I took it and clicked on the number. Then I scrolled down and pressed “Block.”

“There. He doesn't have any power unless we give it to him.”

CHAPTER 34

Career Expo

The day of the expo finally arrived. It was May 7, six long weeks since I had arrived for my first day at PS 23, Ivy Park. This morning, Zoe didn't have to wake me up. I had already been up for hours, finishing my display.

Thump, Thump, Thump.

"Arcade!"

I ran over to the door and flung it open. "Yeah, Zoeeeeeeeee. What's uuuuup?"

She jumped back and waved her hand in front of her nose. "I have one word. Mouthwash."

"And I have two for you. Fashion Consultant."

"Oh, come on! I look great. Which is more than I can say for those socks."

I had chosen my favorites for this Friday—the black with pink flamingos to match my backpack. I wore them to celebrate that I had finally found my passion, my perfect career path!

Well, hopefully.

It had come to me a couple of weeks earlier when I was

over at the Tolleys' checking out the progress of the zipline and the Junk Fit Gym. Casey and Kevin had finally decided to work together so they could both have great displays, and they planned to arm wrestle for the trophy if they tied . . .

"I'm glad you moved here, Arcade," one of them had told me. I still couldn't tell them apart. "You really helped me a lot. I didn't think I could do all this."

The other one agreed. "Yeah, some people think we're just dumb guys and write us off. But you gave us some guidance. You're pretty cool for a goofy-lookin' kid."

Ivan happened to be there too. "Yes, Arcade great counselor!" Then he put his hand on my shoulder. "And best friend. I save seat with coat. Everyday."

My jaw dropped. "What? Is *that* what the coat was for?"

Ivan nodded. "Yes. Not for warmth. For friend. And counselor."

Iron sharpens iron.

That sealed the deal. I went straight to Ms. Weckles, who got me the books I needed for my project. And I was sure Mr. Dooley would approve.

Team Triple T was pretty pumped too.

Bailey cracked her knuckles when I told her. "Took you long enough."

"Food goes great with your career!" Of course Doug would think that.

Amber just smiled and made that baby clap with her hands. "I guess if you're not going to be a veterinarian, this is a good alternative." Then she winked, which made me feel weird.

Zoe waved a hand in front of my eyes. "Yo, sloth bear, quit zoning! You don't want to be late to the expo, do you?

"Nah, I don't. Hey, you think Dad left some notes?"

We raced down the stairs and dove for the notes on the table. We wrestled around for a minute, and finally fell on the floor, gasping for air and laughing. We opened the notes.

I bowed to Zoe. "You go first."

She began to read.

> *Dear Zoe,*
> *Keep shining your light in the right direction, and others will follow.*
> *Love, Dad*

And then I read mine.

> *Dear Arcade,*
> *You're never stronger than when you are helping someone in need. I'll see you at the expo.*
> *Love, Dad*

"Hey! Dad's coming to the expo!"

Zoe was laying on her stomach, looking at her phone.

"Zoe?"

She held it up. "So is *he*."

"What?" I crawled over and read the text from another unknown number.

Today at 3:00.
Bring my token.

Zoe and I narrowed our eyes and stuck our chins out so we looked real tough. Then we said it at the same time:

"Block!"

It took all morning to set up our displays inside the school gym. Some of the kids had been bringing materials throughout the week, especially Kevin Tolley, who had all those milk jugs to carry. Team Triple T's designated area was the farthest back, right under the basketball hoop.

Bailey turned out to be an awesome event planner. Somehow, she got some businesses to donate PVC pipe and vinyl banners with "Team Triple T" printed on them. We assembled the PVC in a square frame and zip-tied the banners to it, which made a super-cool backdrop for our display tables.

At noon, we took a short break for lunch, but then got right back to work.

"ARE YOU ALL READY FOR THE KIDS?" Mr.

Dooley rubbed his palms together. "THIS IS EXCITING! IT'S GOING TO BE DIFFICULT FOR THE JUDGES TO DECIDE ON A WINNER."

"Oh no!" Amber yelled.

"What's wrong?" I put the flyers I was holding down on my table and walked over to where she was listening to a message on her phone.

"Officer Brandon and Cody can't come today! They got caught up in some kind of situation." She sighed. "Oh, wait . . ." She put her hand up while she listened some more. "They're going to send another pair. Whew. I really want the kids to see the dog demo with the bite suit. It's pretty incredible, Arcade. You missed seeing it when we all went to the K-9 academy."

"Did you say *bite* suit? That sounds terrifying."

"It's worse if you're a criminal or a thief *without* a bite suit."

I shivered.

We worked for a few minutes more, and Mr. Dooley finally opened the gym doors.

"THE STUDENTS ARE COMING. NOW'S YOUR TIME TO SHINE."

I stepped back from my table and took a deep breath. My display was simple, not a huge draw, like a zipline, a food truck, or a junk gym. But it represented me, and I hoped the kids would be interested.

The backboard had just one question on it:

Do you like to help people find their way?

There was an answer too:

Be a Guidance Counselor!

I had built a small maze out of cardboard, with a ball in it, so kids could take turns tilting it up and back and side-to-side while blindfolded. And I planned to guide them by giving directions. If they could get the ball to the end, they would earn a piece of candy. And I was going to make sure they *all* made it. And then I had some flyers to give out with information about how guidance counselors help people find their way in life.

Arcade Livingston—Guidance Counselor.

I liked the sound of that.

Someone tapped on my shoulder. I turned, and there she was.

"Ha! I got your back!"

Zoe.

"Hey, don't you have school?" I put my hands on my cheeks. "Did you flunk out?"

"No, I got out early and came to support you." She looked around. "And to keep an eye out for Daisy."

"Do you think that guy can even get in here with all the school security?"

"Probably not. But I'm here just in case."

I checked the time on my phone—1:30. The kids had been coming in, class by class, to check out the displays. There was lots of squealing coming from the zipline, but I was getting my fair share of cheers when a kid got through the maze and won candy.

I was worried about poor Amber, because her K-9 partners hadn't shown up yet.

"They'll be here," I said. "And then you'll have *all* the kids' attention."

Sure enough, five minutes later, they arrived.

It was Officer Frank Langdon, Samson, and an unknown guy wearing a padded jumpsuit.

Amber spotted them coming and grabbed my arm. "Oh no, they're real!"

I tried to calm Amber down by whispering through my smiling teeth. "Just relax. We were adults when they saw us before. They have no idea that we were the surgeons."

Samson ran up to us and wagged his tail. Yeah, he knew.

"Well, it looks like you're the one!" Frank said to Amber.

"The one?" I thought Amber might faint.

Frank pointed to Amber's display backboard. "That says K-9 trainer, right? This must be the place. I'm Frank Langdon, and this is my partner Samson. And this is Officer Seth. He's our suspect for the demo." Frank pointed to the guy in the suit.

"Oh, right. It's so nice to meet you all. I'm . . . Amber. . . . uh, Amber."

Frank chuckled. "Nice to meet you, Amber Amber. Is there a way to gather all the guests for a short demo?"

Amber smiled. "Sure. I checked with Mr. Dooley, and he said we can do it at 2:45, right at the end of the expo. He's going to bring the whole school back to announce the winners so they can all be here to watch."

Frank reached down to pet Samson. "Perfect. For now, we'll hang out by the table and greet the kids."

He didn't have to wait long. A crowd of first-graders arrived and swarmed Samson.

I turned to Amber. "Pretty good display you got there. Glad you're on my team."

She poked me in the chest. "And it wouldn't have happened without you and the help of your token."

Doug had a popular display too. He had chosen just the right food for kids—mini chocolate chip cookie ice cream sandwiches. Bailey had arranged donors for all the supplies, and she had even helped paint the cardboard "truck" in festive colors—oranges, reds, and yellows.

"A good event planner knows her crowd." Bailey was right. Doug's line was so long our whole Triple T team had to get in that cardboard truck and scoop.

"ARCADE, DO YOU HAVE A MINUTE?" I practically jumped out of my shoes. Mr. Dooley was right behind me. I put my scooper down on a plate and stepped out of the cardboard truck.

"Hey, Mr. Dooley! How do you like the expo?" I glanced over at my small display and was happy to see some kids helping others through the maze while I was scooping.

Mr. Dooley crossed his arms and ripped off his glasses. He looked stern. "Here's what I think . . ."

I held my breath.

"I think . . ." He put his glasses back on and grinned. "I think the whole thing is fabulous. And I also wanted to thank you."

"Really? For what?"

"For lighting a fire under those Tolley brothers! They told me that it was you who helped them research their projects, and that gave them the confidence to try something big instead of giving up like they usually do."

I glanced over at the Tolley displays. Kids squealed and giggled as they ziplined a few inches off the floor and tried brick burpees. I could hear Kevin shouting, "Get UUUUUUUP!" and kids shouting the same thing back at him while he mirrored them.

"I like helping people." I decided not to mention that the Tolley twins FORCED me to help them at first.

"And *that* is why I am giving you an A on your project. A guidance counselor is an excellent career choice for you, Arcade. Look around, you're already doing it."

The next hour flew by. Mom and Dad stopped in for a few minutes, and I guided them through my maze.

"I'm proud of you, son," Dad said. "You've always had a gift for helping people, and I know you're going to use that gift in lots of ways here at school and in our new city. I know you didn't want to move, but sometimes we're forced to walk through doors of opportunity for our good and the good of others."

Whoa. He has nooooo idea.

At 2:45, all the classes returned and sat down in rows on the gym floor. Seth stood there in his bite suit while Officer Frank held Samson's leash. "Samson loves kids," Frank explained, "but is trained to catch bad people. So don't be afraid of what you are about to witness."

Then Seth ran from Samson, and Frank yelled something that sounded like "OTT!" Samson tore off after Seth. He leaped and grabbed hold of Seth's arm . . . with his teeth! He tugged and tugged until Seth fell to the ground. Then Samson dragged him around a little.

"Is he biting his arm off?" The little girl in the front row sounded like she was going to cry.

"Platz!" Frank yelled, and Samson let go and ran back to Frank. "Good dog," he said, and he reached down and roughed his neck up.

Everyone in the room clapped. Amber came over and whispered to me.

"What a great dog. I'm so glad we saved him."

After Frank and Samson's demonstration, Mr. Dooley came up to close out the expo. Little kids put their fingers in their ears when he talked.

"OUR SIXTH GRADERS HAVE GIVEN US MUCH TO THINK ABOUT TODAY. THERE ARE MANY JOBS TO CHOOSE FROM WHEN YOU GROW UP. WHILE YOU ARE GROWING UP, THINK ABOUT WHO YOU ARE, WHAT YOU ENJOY DOING, AND WHAT YOU ARE GOOD AT. THEN . . . DO IT!"

"Mr. Dooley is a great teacher," I told Amber. "I'm going to miss him next year when we go to Jr. High."

". . . AND NOW, THE WINNER OF THE EXPO IS . . ."

He smiled, and pointed over to the corner where Scratchy sat, holding an impact wrench, and grinning ear-to-ear.

"JOB SPEEDWAY!"

The Tolleys yelled and beat their chests. I cheered with Team Triple T as we finished snacking on the leftover cookies and ice cream. Job Speedway had beaten us all with their mechanical career choices. They had brought in lawn mowers, scooters, leaf blowers, and someone had even donated and old dishwasher that the kids got to take apart—just to see how it worked. Scratchy wore a jumpsuit that had a name patch that said *Crew Chief Scranton* on it, and his display was all about how to change tires on a race car in less than twelve seconds.

Scratchy came up to receive the trophy and a fun reward for his team: a night of all-you-can-eat pizza and tickets to the local trampoline park. He smiled and scratched his cheek. "Thank you, Mr. Dooley, and PS 23, for this amazing honor. And I want to thank my new friend, Arcade Livingston . . . for giving me the vision to work on a NASCAR pit crew someday."

I clapped loud. "Go, Scratch! Learn to fly a plane next!"

Scratchy raised the trophy in the air. "RADICAL!"

CHAPTER 35

Arcade Livingston: Bone Crusher

The bell rang, echoing throughout the gym. The expo was over.

"TIME TO GOOOOOOO!" Mr. Dooley headed for the door, and we all grabbed our things and raced out after him, excited to enjoy the weekend. Zoe helped me carry my backboard and I took the cardboard maze. There was no candy left.

We stood outside the school.

Zoe checked the time on her phone. "Three-twenty. Guess our thief doesn't have the power to tell time either." She frowned. "I'm sorry about all those library books being lost."

"It's okay. I'll just have to get a summer job so I can pay my fines off. Hey, maybe I'll be a dog surgeon."

We laughed as we walked. And then we saw it roll out from behind some bushes onto the sidewalk.

Daisy.

I dropped the cardboard maze. Zoe put down the backboard. I grabbed for my token, which was as cold as ice.

My heart pounded. Oh, how I wished the token would heat up and get us out of here.

"What should I do, Zoe?"

"Don't ask me! You're the guidance counselor."

A whole bunch of thoughts ran through my mind.

Hang on and enjoy the ride.

Don't be so afraid to strike out that you fail to swing.

He only has power if you give it to him.

"Okay then, I'm going for it."

"And I've got your back."

I remembered the rodeo. That moment was scary for everyone *except* Bone Crusher.

Be a Bone Crusher, Arcade!

That was easier said than done. My palms began to sweat, and my legs felt weak. But my sister had my back. It was now or never.

Swing, Arcade! Just swing!

I stared down at Daisy. Breathed in, breathed out. Imagined a bell ringing, a metal gate clanking open . . .

And I ran for it!

CHAPTER 36

OTT!

The next seconds were a blur. I reached Daisy and grabbed her handle. I ran with her a few steps before someone jumped on my back and tackled me to the ground. I skidded on the sidewalk, scraping skin off my elbows.

"NO! Go AWAY!" I yelled.

"Give it BACK!" A deep voice growled in my ear. "Your mom stole it, and I WANT IT BACK!"

I fought to turn over, and the old guy grabbed for my neck and yanked the token chain.

I pushed his face back with my hands.

"GET OFF ME! It's NOT yours! It has MY NAME ON IT!"

"Let GO OF MY BROTHER!" Zoe punched and kicked the guy from the side, but he wouldn't budge.

He managed to wrestle the token out from under my shirt. He pulled and pulled. At one point, our eyes met. A hood covered his head and part of his face, but he looked familiar. Kinda like that grouchy owner of the mini-golf place in Virginia.

"Give it up, kid!"

I wasn't going to give it up. Nuh-uh! And in that moment, somehow, I knew that no matter how hard he pulled, the arcade token was not going to come off for him. It belonged to me. Just like the old lady had said at the library:

"*Your name's Arcade? Then this is for you.*"

"LEAVE . . . ME . . . ALONE!" I pushed one more time, with all my might.

And then I heard someone else yell, "OTT!"

The next thing I knew, the guy was off me. Fur flew, a dog growled, teeth chomped, and the guy kicked and screamed up a storm. Samson had him by the arm and dragged him away from me, from Zoe, and from the daisy suitcase. I sat up.

"That's DOPE!"

"Run, Arcade!" Officer Frank yelled. "Run *all the way* home! We got this!"

We left the maze and backboard on the sidewalk. But the suitcase full of valuable of library books? No way.

I grabbed Daisy, and we ran all the way back to our apartment.

CHAPTER 37

T-R-U-S-T

Mom and Dad weren't home when we got there. Good thing. I wasn't sure how we would explain, well . . . anything. We both fell down on the living room floor and took a minute to catch our breath.

Zoe rolled on her side to face me. "That—was the scariest moment of my life."

I held the token above my face, twirling it around, watching the gleam come off the Triple Ts.

"Scarier than the *bull*? Scarier than the *plane ride* over New York City?"

"Yep, scarier than all that."

"Zoe, *what* do you think this thing is? And why does that guy think Mom stole it? And who is the mysterious lady I keep seeing? And is that old guy also the shadow?"

She sighed. "You ask too many questions, and I have no answers."

I sat up. "What? Super-smart Zoe? The one who goes to the fancy-pants high school?"

"Yes, even *I* have things to learn. And this is a *really*

weird way to learn things." Zoe got up, pulled Daisy over to the couch, and opened it. "Does everything look intact?"

I searched the contents. There sat my project guide, a big stack of beautiful books, and . . . my phone!

I grabbed it and turned it on. It still had juice.

"Yes, looks like everything is here. Whew."

And then my phone started pinging. Text after text after text came in, all from the same person.

Derek!

And they all said the same thing.

Dude. Call me. I'm in trouble.

My ears got hot, and I hurried to pull up Derek's contact information.

"Derek's in trouble."

Zoe came over next to me. "*Derek*? That must be a mistake . . ."

"Yeah, I know. It doesn't make sense." I pressed the call button, but then my shirt started smoking. I reached in and pulled out the token. The light began to pulse.

Derek answered. "Arcade? What *took* you so long? I'm in trouble!"

"Arcaaaaaaaade . . ." Zoe's eyes popped out as glitter shot down from the ceiling.

Milo bawked. "Triple T! Triple T!"

And the doors appeared. They were transparent again, and this time I could see Derek on the other side. A glittery gold coin slot pulsed back at me.

Zoe put her hands out and shook her head. "Arcade! No! We're already having a rough day. Let's sit this one out!"

"I can't, Zoe! You know what happens if I ignore this thing? It gets harder and harder to pull off the chain, or it burns things up. I have to trust the process. T-R-U-S . . ."

Zoe covered her face with her hands. "I don't understand this!"

I pulled the token from the chain.

"Derek needs my help. Are you coming?"

She stomped her feet a bunch of times. "This *can't* be happening right now! Why did you end up with that crazy token? What are we doing? Why are we in New York? And how many sides *are* on a stop sign?!? AHHHHHHHHH!"

A boatload of glitter dumped all over her.

"There are ten, Zoe. Eight sides, because it's an octagon, *plus* the front side and the back side. You gotta face it, girl. Now . . . are you coming?"

Zoe rolled her eyes and groaned out loud.

"Of course. You know I got your back."

I let go of the token. It found its way into the slot. The pulsing light filled our new house, and I wondered when we'd be back.

Enjoy the ride, Arcade.

I made the open-door motion with my hands, and Zoe linked her arm with mine. The doors parted. We jumped in.

"We doin' this!"

THE END

Discussion Questions

1. *Poof!* You've just been turned into Arcade Livingston, and a pulsing Triple T Token is hanging from a chain around your neck. If you could ride an elevator car into the middle of *any* adventure, what would it be? (Note: You are guaranteed to survive, so pick something daring!)
2. Zoe tells Arcade, "No one enjoys being the new kid." Have you ever been the new kid at school? In youth group? If so, how did the first day go? What went well? Did anything surprise you? What was cool about your new school or meeting?
3. Do you visit the library often? Why or why not? If not, what would it take to get you there? Free candy? Going with a group of friends to work on a project together? If you went, what topics would you most like to research?
4. What do you want to be when you grow up? (Are you staring at those words right now thinking, "I don't even

know what is out there to be?" If so, you're not alone. Arcade didn't know right away either!) Did any of the jobs mentioned in the book interest you? If so, which ones and why?

5. Zoe thinks that Triple T stands for "Transport to Trouble," and Arcade thinks it stands for "Totally Terrific Treasure." What do you think Triple T stands for?" Jot your thought down here (and stay tuned to future books to see if you're right)! Triple T = T ______________ T ______________ T ______________
6. One of Arcade's favorite things to say (besides, "That's dope!") is "That doesn't make sense." Is there anything in your life that doesn't make sense to you right now? What is it? Where can you go or to whom can you go to get answers?
7. Do you have siblings? If so, do you always get along? (Ha! I already know the answer!) Even if you don't always see eye-to-eye, do you have each other's backs? What does that mean and why do you think that might be important?
8. Have you ever had to deal with a bully? What happened? Did a bully ever become your friend? Do you think that's even possible? List a few ways people might be bullying others and not even realize it.
9. Proverbs 27:27 says "As iron sharpens iron, so a friend sharpens a friend." Did Arcade sharpen anyone in the story? Did anyone sharpen Arcade? How do your friends sharpen you? How do you sharpen them?
10. Have you noticed any special talents in your friends? What are they? Can you see them using these talents in

a career someday? If so, tell them! In fact, I dare you to encourage others to use their talents.

11. Are there kids at your school who sit by themselves at lunch? Would you ever consider sitting with them, so you can get to know them better? Why or why not?
12. At Yankee Stadium, big number three tells Arcade, "You can't be so scared of striking out that you don't swing." That makes sense in baseball, but can you apply that wisdom to other areas of your life? Is there something you are scared to do because you are afraid of failing? What is it?
13. Mr. Dooley tells Arcade that he and the other kids in his class were created for a purpose. Do you believe that you were created for a special purpose? What are some of your special interests and talents? Have you ever considered that God gave you those interests and talents to use to make a positive difference in this world?
14. Have you ever passed up an opportunity to go on a new adventure? Why did you pass it up? How is that like Arcade leaving the Triple T Token in his underwear drawer at home?
15. And I *have* to ask you this . . . how many sides *are* on a stop sign? Write your answer here: ____________________
____

Is that your final answer?!?!?!?

Acknowledgments

This series is quickly becoming one of the things I most treasure about my very fortunate and blessed life. I couldn't be who I am without God's most gracious help and wisdom. Many thanks also go to:

My mom Deborah, pops Albert, and brothers Butch and Bryan, and that little kid . . . *You know who you are*—You all have filled my life with enough adventure to write dozens of books like this. Thank you all from the deepest and most intimate place of my heart and soul.

Jill Osborne—The way you stepped into this project with such incredible enthusiasm let me know immediately that you were the writer meant to bring Arcade to life! You took up residence in the part of my mind that refuses to grow up, and you most vividly introduced my inner child to the world.

Keith L. Bell—Your ability to continually dream with me and work with Jill, your creative insights, and your idea, concept, and design of the Triple T Token, and how it relates to "The Coin Slot Chronicles" theme (also your idea), is nothing short of masterful! God has great things in store for you, man!

The Zondervan/Zonderkidz Team—When we first sat down and I shared this idea with you, I had no idea that it would morph into such an amazing opportunity to invite the kids of the world on all sorts of amazing journeys of learning and fun. I truly appreciate you opening this door of opportunity for me!

Every kid who reads this book—I see you. I believe in you. You are amazing. And your own Arcade adventures await you. Go for it! *And always enjoy the ride!*

Read this excerpt from

Arcade AND THE GOLDEN TRAVEL GUIDE

book 2 in the

COIN SLOT CHRONICLES SERIES!

CHAPTER 1

Sideways

"Going up or down?"

The voice blaring over the speaker in the elevator sounds a lot like . . . mine?

Zoe, my older sister who *begged* me not to use the token this time, crosses her arms and leans against the elevator wall.

"Arcade, did you hear that? Are we going *up* or *down*?"

I throw my hands up and stomp a foot. "I don't know! I've never been given a choice before."

I feel for the gold chain around my neck. The Triple T Token is not hanging there because I dropped it in the golden coin slot when glitter began falling from the ceiling and elevator doors appeared in the living room of our apartment.

Yeeeeah. It's been an unusual couple of months in New York City.

Loopy, my Shih-poo, jumps up and scrapes on my leg.

"How did you even get in here, Loopy?" I pick him up and he licks my chin. He has gold and silver glitter stuck to his ears.

"UP or DOWN?" the speaker voice asks again.

"Um . . . Zoe, which is better, up or down?"

"Oh, so NOW you're asking me? No way, bro. I'm not gonna be the one to make the decision that dumps us in the middle of Siberia."

"Siberia? That would be cool! Cold, actually. I read about it in a book once." I pull Loopy in close and rub his neck with my chin.

Zoe rolls her eyes and plops down cross-legged on the elevator floor. "So what's your decision? Up or down?" She flings a hand in the direction of the doors. "All you have to do is push the button."

I check out the elevator wall and my hands turn clammy. "ZOE!!! THERE'S ONLY ONE BUTTON!"

"WHAT?" Zoe jumps up and feels around on all the walls. "Only one button? That figures. The Triple T 'Transport to Trouble' *never* disappoints."

"That's not what the three Ts stand for."

"Then prove it." Zoe sticks out her index finger and pokes the air. "MAKE. A. DECISION."

I stare at the one red button and scratch my head. "This is confusing." Then, an idea hits and goosebumps pop out on my arms. "Hey, you think I could pick *sideways?*"

Zoe waves her arms wildly. "Who knows? There's only one button. Perhaps we could choose diagonal or circular . . . only it's an elevator, Arcade. Elevators only go UP or DOWN!"

"*We*? I thought you told *me* to decide."

Zoe sighs. "Leave it to you to think of something that's *not* one of the choices."

I shrug. "It's worth a try." I take a deep breath. "I choose . . . SIDEWAYS!" I reach out and push the red button.

Immediately, Zoe, Loopy, and I are thrown to the right side of the elevator as it speeds . . . SIDEWAYS!

"OOOF!" I slide down onto the floor, holding Loopy tight. "I don't know where we're going, boy. So when these doors open . . . *if* these doors open . . . don't go running off. These adventures sometimes end in a—"

FLASH!

A bright gold flash fills the car. The elevator screeches to a halt. Zoe, Loopy, and I tumble to the other side and slam against the wall.

"OUCH!" Zoe lies in a heap on the floor.

I blink and wait for the white spots in my vision to clear then push myself up. "I told ya sideways would work."

Zoe straightens her glasses and glares at me. "Looks like we've arrived in Siberia." She tightens the laces on her hot pink high tops and brushes glitter off her black leggings. "Too bad we didn't bring coats." She stands and waits for the doors to open.

DING!

ZONDERkidz™